THE UNICORN HEIST

D.G. Redd

ISBN: 978-0-6453159-6-7

For Liza, Rory, Max, and Rosalie

CHAPTER ONE

Introductions

GROG'S VOICE RUMBLED through the floor of the empty tavern. "You want to steal a unicorn?" He picked at one of his incisors, investigated what he removed, and creased his brow.

Normally the place would be packed with thieves, burglars, and robbers, but not anymore. Defeat weighed against Galan's bones. He sighed. Funnily enough, if you and your compatriots plan all your skulduggery in one place, it tends to scare off all the normal, non-Thieves' Guild-aligned patrons. That's probably why Franki closed up and threw Galan the keys. Now it was just a few upside down chairs on tables, a few barrels stacked behind the bar, the cloying smell of ageing ale, and these last two remnants of the Thieves' Guild.

With a forced smile, Galan ducked around the bar and searched underneath. Grog needed a drink to cheer him up, that was all. They could *both* do with a bit of cheer. It was a human-sized bar, so he couldn't see over the top of it, but it did make it easier to peruse the stock underneath. Where did Franki keep the big mugs, the ones you could sink your sorrows in and drown them for good?

Darkness sat stubborn in every nook and cranny, hiding not just the sorrow-drowning mugs, but the morning after mugs as well. Though Galan preferred the reassuring secrecy of dim-light within which to discuss business matters, the shuttered windows made it next to impossible to find anything down here. How had Franki ever managed to run the place?

He grabbed the single candle burning — all he and Grog could afford — and plunged it into the gaps between shelves. Nothing but plates here. A dead rat there.

"A unicorn must be worth a fair few gold pieces?" Grog said.

Galan glanced up at him. Grog pointed a little further down the bar.

The lone flame burned down the wick, barely an inch of it left, exactly how Galan felt. But, so long as that fire never went out, you could always start up another candle. The trick was in having enough money to afford another candle.

Hot wax dripped onto his fingertip.

They needed enough money for a new candle soon.

"Platinum pieces." Galan found the mugs and opened the tap on a keg. "A fair few *platinum* pieces, my friend." He shuffled his feet back as the first mug overflowed. His soft leather shoe was wet, and would no doubt need to be washed — another expense. Things weren't the same without Franki. He passed the mug to Grog.

The barstool beneath Grog groaned in protest as the half-orc shifted his considerable bulk. "If we can move it."

Galan gave his best, most disarming smile as he poured

his own drink.

"You've got a buyer already?" Grog's prominent brow raised as he took a gulp.

"Yep." Galan climbed up a step stool on his side of the bar. Even then, he could only just comfortably rest his elbows. Grog still towered over him, all muscle and sinew. Nothing in human lands was built with a halfling in mind, not even the pubs.

"Who?"

"An elf lady. I don't know how she found us, what with all the recent... *redundancies* in the guild, but —"

" —Bullshit, Galan. You fired them. Put them out on the street where you got them from."

"Where *we* got them from," Galan corrected. "And with the money we'll get from this job, we can hire everyone back. We can save the guild."

Grog laughed. The floor definitely vibrated. "If you say so. So who is she?"

"Lady Heatherdown of Farrowood."

"Lady who of wha— oh. A druid?"

Galan murmured affirmative sounds while he took a long drink. At least human lands had mugs the right size.

"That explains wanting a unicorn." Grog stroked the tufts of coarse hair that sprouted from his jawline. "Who are we stealing it from?"

"*She* phrased it as an act of liberation." Galan looked down into his ale. "Count Gabriel Radu of Kalindar."

Grog waved his arm wide. "Oh for fuck's sake." He pulled his head back. "You want to steal a unicorn from a vampire?"

"Yep."

"You've come up with some odd ones before. But this

takes the cake."

The beer tasted a little stale. Were you supposed to rotate the kegs or something?

"Alright," Grog relented. "What's the plan?"

Galan hopped off the step, came around the bar, and clambered up his usual stool. He ran his hand along the side of his head, smoothing his long, grey ponytail. When he was done, he flicked a throwing knife into existence and stabbed it into the bar between them. Grog always seemed surprised at how quickly Galan could make a blade appear.

"The Count is having a big party in a few days," Galan said. "He throws one every year. Anyone who's anyone will be there. The big merchants, the royals, government officials; plus all the nobles. Place will be packed. That's when we'll get in." With his finger, Galan drew a line through some spilt ale toward the knife.

"Yeah, right," Grog said. "Go on."

"Next, we steal the unicorn." Galan jabbed his finger at the hilt of the blade. "Then, take it out." He drew another line, away from the dagger.

Grog kept his eyes fixed on the dagger, and the two invisible lines. After a moment he asked, "then what?".

"That's it. We get paid. Get the guild back together."

"I've a few questions." Grog raised his hand. "If you don't mind?"

Though the guild wasn't democratic, Galan always welcomed the input of his second in command. Besides, Galan had only agreed to the job to make sure Grog got a big pay day. No one had stuck with him for as long as Grog had. This bloke had risked everything for Galan's dream. The least he could do was set him up. "Please, please go ahead," he urged, sitting back.

The half-orc started counting details off his meaty fingers. "First, how are we going to get in? Second, where is the unicorn kept? Third, how are we going to transport it? Fourth, how are we going to get it out without being seen? Fifth, what kind of druid has that kind of money?"

Galan suspected that Grog only stopped because he'd run out of fingers on that hand. There was no sense in letting him ask questions about pissing off a vampire.

"Well, my friend," Galan said. "Obviously there are some more *granular* details that we need to work out."

"Yeah, some."

"But that can wait until we've got a crew together."

One of the stacked chairs nearly shook off its table in the onslaught of Grog's ensuing laughter. "Ain't no one who's going to work for us! The whole city knows we've got no money, and no members to get more. I even heard the Merchants' Guild has hired some of our old muscle to protect the business district."

"They're running *our* extortion racket?!"

"Nah, not like that. It's all legal. They're calling it a private guard. And they pay well."

Many years ago, Galan made a promise to Grog that he'd never have to guard another warehouse again. That promise hadn't been broken yet.

"Well there must be a couple of the old players available," Galan said.

"Galan, you're not listening. Even if they were, they don't trust us. We can't really call ourselves a guild anymore. Who's going to pay off the Sentinels to leave well-enough alone? Who's going to ensure our people's families get their share if they get killed?"

Galan gripped the knife and wiggled it free of the bar. If

Franki was here he'd be demanding the Thieves' Guild pay for that new pock-mark. In the end, the tavern was just another victim of the guild's mismanagement. But it was hardly Galan's fault. Running things was a lot harder than larceny and burglary had led him to believe. Maybe with his share of the job he could try starting up the guild again, but without Grog this time. He didn't want to put his friend through it all again...

" —Of course," Grog continued. "There's always Elovar."

Galan hadn't been listening. "No no, fuck no. That cunt will get us all killed."

"What about Vanenas?"

"She's knocked up."

"Elvalor?"

Galan paused for a moment. "Yeah maybe," he said. "Actually, that's not a bad idea. We could get into the party easily with him."

"And the rest of the plan?"

"Lady Heatherdown can deal with the unicorn."

Grog's muscles tensed. "She's coming on the job?"

"Yeah," Galan confirmed. "It was a condition of hers." He continued before Grog could argue. "We'll need a fake unicorn to leave in place."

"A fake unicorn?"

"A horse with a fake horn. We might be able to get out of the city before they notice it's not real."

Grog took a sip. "Only we can't afford a horse."

"Come on" — Galan opened his arms out wide — "we're thieves. We'll steal the horse."

"Where are we going to find a white horse to steal?"

"Why do we need a white horse?" Galan asked.

"Unicorns are white." Grog scratched behind one of his

pointed ears. "I've read about them."

"You read?"

"Also read that their horns can cure anything."

"Is that so? Let's see what Elvalor thinks."

"Righto. Let's get going then. I've got a stop to make, then I'll meet you down at the New Black Dog." Grog rose, walked to the front door and pulled it open. Stark sunlight struck the floorboards. A cockroach dashed into a gap between them.

"No problem, I've got an errand to run myself. I'll see you there." Galan clapped his hands. "Oh, have you still got that bag of holding?"

"Of course."

"Bring it."

"Should we lock up on our way out?"

"Why?" Galan snuffed out the candle, leapt off his stool, and walked into the day. "There's no thieves left in town."

LADY HEATHERDOWN OF Farrowood hated being a druid. She hated the dirt, the grass, the rain, the sun, the moon, the beetles, the birds, the animals, the incessant demands of all creatures, great and small. But most of all she hated that it was the only thing she knew how to do.

The grove was thriving. Birds sang merrily, the little brook bubbled out of the spring, and everything was dappled in the cool shade of the ancient oaks. Oh god the oaks. Biggest, stupidest trees there were. Nothing like a birch or a eucalypt. Try to tell an oak to grow down toward the water table and it just stares at you. Well, at least she didn't need to deal with any willows. She'd probably try and neck herself if she had to hear about how hard *their* lives were.

She sat on a moss-carpeted stone next to the icy water. A fish stared at her from under the current, mouthing something in Fish.

Heather rolled her eyes. "I can't hear you," she told it. She couldn't reply in Fish, because she wasn't in the water, and had no desire to plunge her head in.

It continued opening and closing its mouth. A bubble rose up and broke the surface.

Wow, fish were dumb. No matter how many times she tried to tell them, they just didn't seem to be able to grasp a simple concept like the propagation of waves through changing mediums. She turned away from the water.

Oh, look! Here's a happy little critter taking a shit on the grass. That stuff took a lot of effort to grow just right, and considering how deep and thick it was, it would take a while to clean up the mess.

With a groan of disgust, Heather got up and moved to where the oh-so-cute little bunny had relieved itself. It wasn't so bad. A lot easier than cleaning up after wolves and bears. She bent down and grabbed some leaves.

All of nature's animals did whatever the hell they liked. But not Heather, *no*, and she'd never been given much of a choice in the matter either. She'd done what her parents wanted, was given her grove, and told to tend to it. Scrubbed shit, told plants where to grow, and got insect bites.

Seventy-six years later she was still doing it.

But she had an out now. Oh boy did she. Most druids lived their whole lives eking out a subsistence living until they died from an infected cut or a... mountain lion or something, without ever being called into the council and given a job. Some had been out of contact with the council and other druids for so long they doubted their existence, or so one of the council members had told her gleefully a month ago. She wasn't surprised they'd chosen her, she really was very good at being a druid, but she wished they hadn't.

At first.

But then she learned about the unicorn. A unicorn that had gone missing from its usual forest. Apparently a human had captured it. Not just a human either, but a vampire. One of the most unnatural things that existed. *They didn't die of old age.*

This, of course, upset the council a great deal. And so they wanted her to kill the vampire, and free the unicorn. Their idea was to utilise thieves to steal and then free the unicorn.

But she had other plans.

As she picked up the last of the little poo pellets — good enough for fish to eat — and tossed them into the water, something crunched behind a nearby tree. Heather went to investigate, and found the same white rabbit, hunched over in a sunbeam, munching on her wild-flowers. Did it have any idea how long it took for her to have the trees keep that patch lit for the flowers to grow?

She spoke in Rabbit, a fleeting, irreverent language. "What the fuck are you doing?"

"Eating."

"Yeah, I know. But can you do it somewhere else?"

"No."

A long black leg, thin like a stick, curved around the base of the tree near the rabbit. Minuscule hairs and notched spines bristled along its length.

"Please?" She asked the rabbit.

"No."

Another leg appeared, claw-tipped, with bulging knuckles at the joints.

Heather grimaced. "Please? You know you're like, a prey-animal, right?"

"No. I'm busy. Leave me alone."

A narrow thorax followed the legs, with two fat pedipalps questing silently at the front, then a bulbous abdomen. A single red stripe extended from the back of the eight eyes all the way to the spineret. Heather shivered. It was far larger than the rabbit, its legs appeared much too weak to hold up the weight of it. How was something so horrifying *natural*?

"Ugh," Heather groaned at the sight of her animal companion. Nothing made her feel more uneasy than when it hovered around her. And it was always nearby, just sitting there, waiting for her to see it.

She turned away just as it struck, no doubt ensnaring the rabbit with its many limbs and striking over and over again with its fangs. The rabbit wouldn't be killed right away, it would die slowly, its insides turned to jelly. Then Legs would feed, probably before the bunny was dead, drinking the internal organs.

Oh well, it was all a part of the natural world. Nothing she could have done about it.

On the other side of the grove, far away from Legs and his feast, she gathered what she'd need for the journey. The satchel bag she'd found a few decades ago on a corpse nearby — some wayward traveller who ventured too far from the road — was a must. A couple handfuls of berries. Some dried fruits. What else?

She'd need a wooden stake, just in case the vampire didn't cooperate, though she hoped it wouldn't come to that. It probably would. And based on what the halfling in charge of the Thieves' Guild had told her, they might run into some trouble, so she'd need a weapon too.

Regretting the inevitable questions, she rose and placed her hand against a nearby oak.

"Make me a wooden stake and a quarterstaff," she asked it. "Please."

Why? Are you going out again? Guys! She's going again!

Where?

Please don't go, we need you here!

Can you bring us back something?

She hated oaks. "I'll be back soon. I'm going on official druidic council business."

Really? What kind of business?

"If you must know, a vampire has captured a unicorn."

Oh no!

Oh, could you imagine?

A vampire unicorn! That would be horrible!

"Right, I know. Very unnatural. So you can see why I need the stake and quarterst—"

The two items landed in the leaves nearby. She broke off contact with the trees before they said more and checked out her new equipment. The stake was short, stout, and sharp. The quarterstaff was tall, with just the right amount of give in it; a solid weapon.

Without offering any more information to the trees, she jammed the stake into her satchel, and strapped the quarterstaff to her back with a spare strip of leather. She didn't look back as she made her way past the edges of her grove. If everything went according to plan, she'd never return.

Sentinel Janu read over the report a second time, then a third. Ainsworth, a striking young human, stood at attention in the small space between Janu's desk and the office door. He had a good head on his shoulders, a strong sword-arm, and so far knew when to shut up. A good addition to the Sentinels, but a little too straight-laced to be her adjutant. She could fix that.

There were a lot of words on the parchment, but she thought she had the gist of them. She'd got this far in the Sentinels without knowing her words and letters, why did she need to learn them now? "You're sure about this?"

"Yes, Janu."

"Hm." Janu leaned back from the stacks of paper on her desk. Report after report filed into her office, and report after report filed back out. While she'd welcomed the promotion's bump in pay, she never would have accepted it if she knew how far it would take her from the streets. Instead of cracking heads in the slums of Threerun, she was now cracking open fresh pots of ink deep in the headquarters, without even a window to see the people she was protecting. How did this administrative bullshit help anyone?

Shuffling old Captain Tenn out and putting her in charge was probably a means to keep her away from the real action. The city council had long complained about her tactics, but they had no idea how to get things done. That was why Captain Tenn had given her the option to join instead of facing prison in the first place; she knew the underbelly and how it worked.

With a wave of her hand, a quill rose from the desk, meandered past a nest of burning candles, and met with her fingers. She scrawled her signature — a vague resemblance of letters — across the bottom of the report and flicked the sheet to Ainsworth. He snatched it from the air and left without another word, leaving the door open. A fairly standard reaction from a human to a gnome's inherent magic. That good head of his would soon get used to it. It would have to if he was to remain her right-hand man.

She folded her arms and frowned. The Thieves' Guild was finished, so said the report, its last members gone. Now only Galan and Grog remained, which, all things considered, meant she had finally won. No longer would they plague Threerun, preying on the weak, treading over whatever little hope there was left in the downtrodden.

But it didn't feel like a victory. Sure, it was her order that had the city gates sealed and the slums raided. And it was her order that had it repeated on a random day every week for months. But she wasn't down there, kicking in the doors, arresting the criminals, sweeping out the filth. According to all reports, the payments she'd authorised for the informants had been the final deciding factor, but it wasn't really... right. Finishing off the guild deserved more than that.

The headquarters' lack of windows and constant warm glow of candlelight was normally more than tolerable, it was preferential, reminding her of the burrows she was born in. But now she needed to get out, stretch her legs. Do something meaningful, not this bullshit administration.

With a little jump, she hopped off the overly tall seat and rummaged through the equipment next to her desk. When she was promoted, she'd requested a gnome-sized workstation. Twelve months later, she was still barely able to see the opposite wall from this side of the table. Gods-be-damned administration bullshit.

After securing her leather armour — replete with yellow Sentinel rose — and fastening her sword belt, she swept into the hallway. By her order it was dim down here, the stonework lit by only sporadic candles so as to suit her gnomish eyes over the other Sentinels.

Clean air breezed in, smelling of the horses and market

foods outside, a result of some changes she'd ordered from the human masons. They'd managed to construct buildings large enough to have subterranean areas, but couldn't see how to engineer necessities like airflow or fresh water. The latter was something she was still trying to convince them of, hopefully the new promotion would help.

As she made her way to the stairs at the end of the hallway, a voice called out from one of the many rooms that lined it.

"Janu?"

It was Marrid Burnstone. One of the only other non-humans in the Sentinels, and one of the only dwarves outside the mountain homes that wasn't a drunken exile. He was here as a sort of diplomat, sent due to recent rumblings of war between the dwarves and elves. But the nuance of the position was lost on the dwarven kings, so they sent a warrior. Without any interest in politics or courtly proceedings, he found his most effective use was down here with the Sentinels.

The recent expulsion of criminals from Threerun couldn't have been done without his help.

"What is it, Marrid?"

She stepped back as he exited his office, straightening the shirt under his usual polished plate armour. His long brown hair was plaited and secured tightly behind his head, beard gathered and weighed down by metallic beads. Janu was a little surprised to see Marrid's battleaxe leaning against the desk behind him; the first time she'd seen him in any way unprepared for a skirmish.

"I've just received a report I think you should read." He waved a sheet of parchment at her. What could be described as a smile cracked across his face. "Says that the Thieves'

Guild is no more."

Of course he already knew, most reports crossed his desk before they reached hers. He'd become a sort of gatekeeper of her attention. "I've seen it," she said.

He held a meaty hand out to her. "Well then, Janu. Congratulations."

That explained why he wasn't carrying the war axe. She shook it. "Thank you, Marrid."

"You don't seem too happy with this result, Janu?" He raised an eyebrow.

"Mission accomplished, right?"

He folded his arms and twisted his bottom lip to the side. "If a little anticlimactic. Oh I would've liked to have been there, in the final moments."

Janu nodded. "Only there was no final moment. They just sort of... fizzled out."

As the two of them stood in silence, Ainsworth bounded down the stairs at the end of the passage. He stopped and peered forward, no doubt seeing their two vague shapes in the half light. After a few moments he came forward and snapped a salute.

"Sentinel Janu. Sentinel Burnstone. We've received word from one of our informants."

"Go on." Marrid returned the salute. Janu noted that he'd stopped correcting the other Sentinels about his non-official status.

Ainsworth set his feet apart and put his hands behind his back. He kept his eyes forward, seeing over their heads. "The Thieves' Guild has organised a new job, sirs."

Janu studied her adjunct. "With just the two of them?"

"Yes, sir. Our informant says they're looking to steal a unicorn from Count Gabriel Radu of Kalindar."

Marrid sucked his teeth. "Oh, that's not a good idea."

"No, it's not," Janu said. "It's a bold move. How much is a unicorn worth?"

"Several hundred platinum coins." Ainsworth said.

How the hell would *he* know how much a unicorn was worth? If Ainsworth was right, that would be enough to reignite the Thieves' Guild, keep it running for years. No doubt it would attract new blood.

"Looks like it's not over yet?" Marrid asked Janu.

This was nothing but an opportunity. "I want everything you know on my desk in an hour," she informed Ainsworth.

Finally, she had something worth doing; but there was still one problem.

"Marrid," she said. "I want you to recall and reassign everyone working on the Thieves' Guild. It's clear they can't be trusted to get things done. I'll take this over personally."

"Recall *all* of them?"

"Yes." She turned back to Ainsworth, who still stood rigid over them. "I want the identity of that informant too. I'll interrogate them further myself."

"Sir?" Ainsworth's eyes darted down to hers then snapped back up. "Sentinel rules state that I cannot inform you of the informant's name."

Life was so much easier on the streets, whether in her previous life as an orphan stealing food, or her new one as a Sentinel stopping crime. The only rules that applied to you were the ones people saw you breaking. If Ainsworth had half as good a head as she thought, he'd give her the informant's name eventually. It could wait.

"Go and find what Galan and Grog are up to next then."

"Yes, sir!"

When both Marrid and Ainsworth had left to go about their tasks, she smiled. Finally. Something meaningful to do.

CHAPTER TWO

Plans

THERE WAS SOMETHING to be said about the New Black Dog Tavern, at least Galan thought so. It was a lavish place, despite its less than reputable location, which gave it an oddly curious charm for the more well-to-do. It towered over its neighbours, a full three stories tall, its stone pillars and archways making a mockery of the other buildings. Potted ferns stood outside the wide, ornate wooden doors, beside which stood two smartly dressed, unarmed bouncers.

Galan shifted his weight and leaned against a storefront across the street. "He's definitely playing today?" Galan asked Grog beside him.

Wood creaked as the half-orc pressed himself up off the shop. "Every day this week. Only the finest for the New Black Dog."

"Hm." Galan folded his arms. "Is Riley working today?"

"Yeah."

"Right. Well. When we see him, we'll go over and say hello, see if he can't get us in."

"Why don't we just wait for Elvalor to finish for the day and speak to him then?"

That was an option, of course. But the druid said she'd be outside the city at sunrise tomorrow morning. The last thing they needed was to lose their best chance of saving the guild, and Galan's best chance to make right by Grog, due to tardiness. Besides, Galan only had a few coppers left. They'd need money for provisions and gear. He could pull a decent grift inside.

"Come on, Grog. There's good times in there. Good money."

"Easy marks."

"Exactly."

The building shifted a little as Grog slumped back against it. Galan rolled his hand around and produced a knife, smiled at Grog's astonishment, and began flipping it around his fingers. He was good at this, good with his hands. When he first arrived on these shores he got started with a simple shell game. No one in the Three Kingdoms had seen anything like it.

"You remember when we met, Grog?" Galan stopped the point of the knife on his fingertip and balanced it there. "And I told you we could build a bustling business of our own? Remember what you told me?"

Grog used a finger to clean out his pointed ear. "Yeah. I told you that if you didn't pull it off, that I'd pull your arms and legs off."

"But I pulled it off, didn't I?"

"You did. So you still have your arms and legs."

Galan laughed, though to be honest, he was never really sure with Grog. "Right. Well, we're back to where we started."

"Only I'm not in the city guard anymore."

"You're missing the point, Grog. We're back to our roots, getting things done, building ourselves up. It was too easy at the top. We got soft."

"Speak for yourself, Galan. I liked being at the top. Things was easy. Now we're down here trying to talk our way into a tavern. We can't get much lower than this."

There wouldn't be any convincing Grog, he didn't understand the thrill of their chosen profession. But why do anything if you didn't enjoy it? Grog's time in the guild was coming to an end, even if he was too proud to admit it. The second in command of the Thieves' Guild deserved to walk away with more money than he could ever spend.

"Look," Grog said. "There's Riley."

Across the road, a tall half-elf emerged from the front doors and spoke with the bouncers. He was dressed in well-made, functional clothes, much like how Galan himself dressed. The sort of garb you could wear anywhere and never look too far out of place. Riley spotted them watching him, said a few more words to the bouncers, and then crossed the street.

"Galan. Grog," Riley said, all business. "What are you here for?"

As usual, Galan spoke for both himself and Grog. "Just looking to play a game of cards is all. Think you can let us in?"

Riley scratched at his thin goatee and chuckled. "Been a long time since you two needed to work a card table, hasn't it?"

"True," Galan said. "Times are tough all round. We'd be grateful."

"Grateful? Throw me twenty percent."

Grog unfolded his arms. "That's double what it should be, Riley." There was no threat in his tone, but his bulk didn't require it.

"Yeah," Riley said. "But times are tough." He gave them an exaggerated wink.

They didn't have many options. Even a year ago, when the guild was a force in Threerun, getting into the New Black Dog Tavern wasn't easy. Whoever funded the place had deep pockets. Deep enough to pay off everyone Galan sent to straighten the situation out. Even Grog. At the end of the day, you joined the Thieves' Guild to make money. It didn't matter much how you got it.

"Alright," Galan said. "Fifteen percent." He still had a reputation to uphold, twenty percent was highway robbery.

Riley flashed perfect, white teeth. "For old time's sake I'll take fifteen. Come on."

Once they were through the doors, Riley left them to their business. The majority of the ground floor was open, separated into different sections by two imposing columns of stone. The polished wooden floors stepped up the wall opposite the entrance to a balcony that overlooked everything. No doubt it was from up there that Riley would survey the bar and the gaming tables, making sure there was only ever enough riff-raff to keep things exciting for the wealthy patrons. Six elaborate chandeliers hung from the ceiling, boasting more lit candles than Franki's pub would've burned in a week. Serving girls wound their way throughout it all, ferrying drinks and meals a cut above what the surrounding neighbourhood deserved.

A sharp burst of music accentuated Galan and Grog's entrance. Next to the stairs was a low stage, upon which several musicians plucked and strummed and harmonised.

Elvalor was front and centre, vocalising in his Elvish tongue and playing his lute. It was a pleasant enough tune, but nowhere near lively enough for a tavern. But Galan had to admit, the reserved nature of the music seemed fitting for a place like this.

"Come on, Grog," said Galan, answering the call of the gaming tables. "Let's work some pigeons at the cards."

With a little jangle, Grog reached into the bag of holding on his belt and produced a handful of coins, only one was silver, the rest copper. Galan took them and added his own to the pile. Less than half a gold coin's worth between them. No matter, they didn't need much to get started.

At this time of day, the place wasn't busy, but there were a few full tables. Mostly the well-tailored sons of merchants, a few girlfriends brought along to witness their beau's casual comfort in a lower-class establishment. Everyone was playing Riddish, which wasn't a surprise, it was an easy game to gamble on. Unfortunately for these rich pigeons, it was an easy game to scam them on too.

Galan sat at the only table with an elderly woman. Old rich ladies were the easiest. A bit of cheeky banter and they were almost *happy* to lose their money. She had her poorest clothing on, which no doubt cost more to have made than the coins he held in his hand. Both her and two men bid him a pleasant day as he sat down, their eyes sparkling with expectation.

Grog continued on to the bar just beyond the table and ordered himself a drink. He produced another couple of coppers from his bag. That was the first time Grog had ever held back money from Galan. At least since they started the guild. He didn't blame his friend for keeping a secret nest-egg, they all did, but it couldn't be worth much. Galan would pad it out for him soon.

"Morning gentlemen." Galan turned his frown into a quick smile. "What's the game?"

One of the men, sporting a red beard and tired eyes replied. "Riddish. Four card draw, two card river. Split hands if you need to."

"Split hands works fine for me." Galan spoke in a slightly accented voice to give himself a little more of a tough street character. "What's the ante?"

"Two bits," replied the other man from under his hat. It was funny the types of things rich people considered 'lower class', but keeping your hat on indoors wasn't too far off the mark. "If you got 'em."

Galan let the coins in his hand clink together. "Looks like I won't be playing long." He tossed two silvers into the centre of the table. Only a fistful of coppers to bet with now. It would be enough. Surely.

If not, maybe Grog had a few more coins stashed away.

The others threw their silver in.

The old woman spoke as she dealt the cards. "What's your name, sir?"

"Galan Leafwhisper, ma'am." Galan gave the best awkward little bow he could. He didn't ask her name in return, and instead focused on the cards.

"I am Lady Vars. These two gentlemen are Messrs Vars, my children."

'Messrs'? He'd have to ask Riley what that meant later. "Well, good day to you three," Galan said.

The Messrs Vars mumbled greetings and then eagerly picked up their cards. Galan fumbled his own cards as he picked them up. If he made them think he'd had a little too much to drink, they might think he'd be a little too brash with his bets.

Luck was on his side, he held four suitors.

"Three coppers," Hat Vars said.

"I'll spot that," Beard Vars said.

"Spot and raise," Galan said, tossing his copper coins in. "Two cuts." He laughed internally at the surprise and delight on their faces. That colloquialism was made up on the spot, but it had drawn them right into the theatrics of it all.

Lady Vars took a moment before replying. "I'll spot."

Both brothers did the same. Then Lady Vars dealt two cards face up in the middle of the table, a green six and a blue consort. They gave Galan nothing, but his four suitors were cards enough.

"I'll split," Galan said.

The others nodded but offered no more bets. Shame, but he likely had the strongest hands. There wasn't much anyone could do with a six and a consort off colour. Galan revealed his four cards.

Lady Vars gasped as she tossed her hand to him. "Oh you are a lucky one," she said.

Messrs Vars threw their cards down as well. Galan leant forward, and with his forearm, pulled the money and loose cards toward him. After stacking the coins, he palmed two of the suitors while he squared up the deck. They'd come in handy later.

Galan started dealing before everyone had put their ante on the table. He now had an ace and a king, with some off colour numbers. He always considered himself lucky. If a queen came out first on the flop, he could deal out one of the palmed suitors second and have a full run.

"Six coppers," he announced.

"Spot," Hat Vars said.

The Beard Vars took a good long time before folding.

Lady Vars took no time in throwing her hand in. Either they had terrible cards or Galan was being too aggressive.

Grog was still at the bar, paying them no mind but keeping an eye out. His hulking presence always made Galan feel safe when cheating people out of their money.

As the first flop card revealed itself to be a queen, Galan slipped a suitor from his sleeve and dealt it out.

"Six coppers," he said.

Hat Vars fiddled with the coins in front of him, then studied his cards. He gave a furtive glance to Lady Vars before replying. "Spot," he said, pushing a small stack of coins forward.

Galan smiled and revealed his cards. The three Vars leant back in their chairs and groaned.

"You have the devil's own luck!" Lady Vars cried, laughing.

"What brings you down this way?" Galan asked the group while he pocketed some more useful cards. "If you don't mind me saying so, this area of town doesn't see your kind too often."

Lady Vars smiled and took in the room. "No, but the Black Dog has its charms."

The next hand wasn't salvageable, so Galan folded early. "And what is it that you do, Lady Vars?"

"Oh, I'm a merchant. I deal in... let's just say *exotic* goods, for discerning clientele."

That wasn't what Galan was expecting. Especially considering that up until very recently he was in receivership of protection money from all three brothels in town. How long had she been operating without the Thieves' Guild's approval?

"How long have you been in that business?" Galan tried

to make it sound like casual conversation.

"A good many years now," Lady Vars replied.

No wonder the guild collapsed, people hadn't been doing their jobs. He raised an eyebrow at Grog, but the half-orc was busy looking busy watching the band. Seemed like no one was doing their job.

The next hand came out. Two suitors, two kings. Depending on the flop, he could split his hand, and with the cards up his sleeve he had a good chance of winning.

When it was Galan's turn to bet, he placed his coppers in the centre of the table. "Spot."

Lady Vars dealt out two queens. With a split, identical hand, both runs, Galan almost certainly had the win.

"Three silver." Galan slid more coins in.

The two sons folded. Lady Vars rearranged the cards in her hand and frowned at them.

"Three silver," she declared. "And I'll raise you a gold coin."

Galan made a show of glancing over his coins, but he already knew he didn't have enough to cover it. "I'm afraid you've tapped me out, madam." He needed the money, and his hand was a winner. "But if you're willing to take my money on credit, I will spot you."

Lady Vars laughed a silent breath and looked at her two sons. "Very well," she said. "But I warn you, I intend to collect on your debt."

"I assure you, I'll pay you any money I owe," Galan said. "If you're comfortable with it, I'd be happy to raise you as well, five gold pieces."

Grog shifted at the bar and caught Galan's eye. He gave a short shake of his head. Maybe he had been paying attention.

"Oh well...," Lady Vars placed her cards face down on

the table. She looked at her two sons, both of them shrugged. "Yes. Yes! Then I'll spot the five."

One of her sons placed the coins in front of her.

Galan rolled his cards down on the table. Gold glinted with the promise of new riches as he leaned forward to collect his winnings.

The red bearded son reached a hand out to stop him. "Hold on a moment," he said. "You haven't seen her cards yet."

Lady Vars held two kings and two aces. "Oh! That was exciting." She clapped her hands together.

From nearby, Riley walked over after a signal from Hat Vars. Had he been waiting there? Beard Vars still hadn't let go of Galan's hand. Grog raised a questioning eyebrow but Galan signalled him not to interfere. It was unlikely they'd get out of here alive by starting a fight.

"Yes, Lady Vars," Riley said. "How may I be of service?"

"Do you know this halfling?"

"Yes, madam."

"He owes me six gold coins. See to it that it's noted in the Merchants' Guild register."

Riley gave a short bow. "Of course, Lady Vars."

Since when were the Merchants' Guild in the business of prostitution? Unless they'd opened registry notifications to everyone... but that would upset the Bankers' Guild and hamper commerce. Something didn't add up...

"Owe a bit of money do you?" Elvalor spoke in a sing-song voice, the kind of voice well-off humans believed elves used. He wore nice clothes, light and well-fit, probably the best he owned. After a quick look to Grog, he ran his hand through his short, dark hair. "Might put you in a spot of trouble with the wrong crowd."

Galan hadn't heard the music stop, or seen the elf's arrival.

"Seems that I do," Galan replied.

Elvalor dropped seven gold coins on the table, into a little stack, and dropped the voice. "I'll cover it, Lady Vars," he said. "Galan here isn't worth the trouble. Quite a serious guy he is."

"Is that so?" said Hat Vars.

"It is so," Grog said from behind them.

Galan gave a curt nod as he rose from the table, then followed Elvalor to the far side of the tavern. Grog waited a moment before he too joined them.

"Do you have any idea who she is?" Elvalor released the knot holding his collar up. He signalled the barman for three drinks.

"No," Galan admitted. "But she cheats at cards. She had the two aces. *I* had the two aces up my sleeve."

Grog's chuckle rumbled as he leaned over to lift his drink. "Must have been an Orthendine deck. In any case. We're still in need of some coin."

"You haven't got any more?" Galan asked, taking a sip. "You had—"

"—Just enough to buy a drink is all," Grog finished.

It had been a long time since Galan's friend had looked that imposing.

"Let's not let bad times turn us against each other," Elvalor said. "What are you guys doing here?"

Galan smiled. "We've got a job that needs a way into a high society function up in Kalindar. Figured you'd be game."

"I figured you were here for me, and I may be persuaded," Elvalor said. "What's the take?"

"It's a lot. More than playing in a joint like this." Galan

took another sip.

"I get paid quite well here. How much?"

"One thousand gold pieces," Galan said. "Thereabouts."

Elvalor gulped his drink down. "Alright, count me in."

"You don't want to know what it is?" Grog asked.

"For that kind of money?" Elvalor shrugged. "Nope."

"Do you know what colour unicorns are?" Galan asked.

Elvalor frowned. "I'd never put much thought into it, why do you ask?"

"RECRUITING ELVALOR?" SENTINEL Janu mused. "Now *that* is interesting. He's a swindler isn't he?"

Heat from the stone wall seeped into her shoulder blades, helping to release some of the tension that had plagued her since the promotion. The Sentinel headquarters was a large building, partially attached to the larger government one, though truth be known, the Sentinels had taken over the underground sections of both. Everything was hard rock and stout timber, without a hint of artistry or cheer. Even a bright, sunny day seemed powerless to do anything other than heat the rock.

Ainsworth kept himself at attention. "Yes, sir. Elvalor can talk his way through anything, sir."

"Count Radu is hosting a party soon." Marrid ran his hand through his beard and squinted against the day. "I got an invite as a diplomat." He practically spat the last word. "They might be thinking of talking their way in."

"Yes, that's right," Janu said. "Radu has a big party every year. Invites the Queen, all the councillors, mayors, everyone with any power. There's been a few missing persons cases we've been told to drop on account of the investigation getting too close to him. He makes friends with all the right people. Fucking vampires."

"Sir?" Ainsworth asked. "If I may, sir?"

"Stand at ease, Ainsworth." If he was going to remain in position as her right-hand man, he'd need to cut the rigid bullshit. "Just say your piece."

Ainsworth slumped slightly, but his feet remained shoulder-width apart and his hands remained clasped behind his back. "Elvalor is, among less desirable things, a well known musician. A party like the kind Radu hosts would need several troupes. That could be their ticket in."

"Good work, Ainsworth." Janu had already made the connection, but wanted to reward his quick thinking with some acknowledgement.

Marrid shifted his weight and watched Janu. "Are you sure you're the right person to be taking charge of this investigation?"

Didn't that just take the piss? "Who better? Need I remind you that you're not technically a Sentinel?" She hoped that barb stuck.

"I may not be," Marrid said. "But this is only one of many problems the Three Kingdoms face. There's plenty enough for us to do here in Threerun. Your attention may be better spent elsewhere."

It was good Marrid didn't rise to the bait. Janu doubted she would've been able to do much if he decided to take offence. She needed to reel it in a bit more, his attention to detail and his help had been much needed this past year. No need to get reckless.

"No." Janu's tone left no room for debate. She rose up from the wall. "I'll see to this personally. I want that guild done away with."

"There's no guild there anymore," Marrid said. "Besides,

you know something else will just take its place."

Who did he think he was? She had seen the rise and fall of more criminal enterprises than any of these well-bred arseholes. And she had been a part of more of them than she'd ever admit. But those times were past, she wasn't a starving orphan on the streets anymore.

"Then we'll take the next one out as well," she said.

Ainsworth still stood over them.

"What is the mission of the Sentinels?" she asked him.

"To keep the Three Kingdoms safe, of course." Ainsworth's chin rose up even higher, his jaw set even tighter.

"And that's what I'm going to do. Now." She slumped back against the stonework, ending the debate. "We've got two founding members of the Thieves' Guild, the last two members, recruiting a musician on a job to steal a unicorn. From a vampire's party. Do we know what they plan to do with the unicorn?"

"That is a little unclear." Ainsworth shifted on his feet, not quite settling back into the same ramrod straight stance as before. "All my informant knows is that a druid of some description is paying for the theft. Lady Heatherdown. We have no files on her, she's not a known denizen of the cities."

Marrid's nose whistled. "This druid probably wants the unicorn freed from captivity." He tilted his head up to the sky and scratched under the braids at the back of his head. "Does that count as a theft?"

"Doesn't matter," Janu said. "Count Radu is in possession of it. If they take it, it's theft. I don't give a shit about animal rights. Can we get someone onto this druid, see what she's about?"

"There's no need, sir." Ainsworth visibly swallowed.

"They're going to meet her tomorrow morning, outside the city."

These criminals moved quickly. "Great, then we can put a tail on her," Janu said. "Any other info from your informant?"

"No, sir. But, well... I'm not sure if we can trust the informant."

No shit you couldn't trust an informant, they were all crooks. Maybe Ainsworth didn't have such a good head on his shoulders?

"Who is it?" Janu asked.

"Sir?"

"The informant. Who is it?"

Marrid held his palm up for peace. "You know he's not allowed to tell you, Janu," he said. "Don't put the poor man on the spot."

All of these rules did nothing except bind the Sentinels. The councilman and philosophers decreed the laws, themselves having never stepped in the knee-high filth of these streets. If they'd known only a fraction of the crime that slithered through the city below them they would never hold Janu back.

The rules that shackled her — more so as a Sentinel than they did in her old life — weren't something she could fight, only bend when needed. This wasn't one of those times, at least not yet. When time soaked and weakened Ainsworth's rigid beliefs, she'd find out who the informant was. And then she'd use that knowledge as leverage to bring Galan and the guild to a permanent end.

Threerun couldn't take much more of the criminal underbelly rotting her from within.

"Fine," she said, turning away. "That's enough for now.

Get some sleep, and gather your gear. Have someone keep a watch on Galan and co to let us know if they move out earlier than expected. You'll both sleep here tonight so we're not running around getting our shit organised when it's time to follow."

A gaggle of shoeless, dirty children ran past. Orphans. No matter how much of her stipend she handed to them, they were never any better off. It took more than charity to prevent the exploitation and abuse she lived through. A firm, decisive backhand across the face of criminality was what it needed.

But even still, no matter how many criminals she arrested, things were getting worse. The Thieves' Guild had to be put down. So long as Galan was still around, so was the guild.

"Shouldn't we send word to Kalindar?" Marrid asked. "Let Radu or the Sentinels up there know what's happening?"

"No," Janu said. "Galan will get wind of any suspicion. He always does. We'll follow at a distance, keep an eye on them. There's going to be more to this heist, we need to know what."

"What should I—we pack?" Ainsworth asked.

Janu rolled her eyes. "You know... adventuring gear. Shovel, bedroll, lantern. A sword. That kind of thing."

"Yes, sir."

"Oh," Janu raised a finger. "Bring some of those teleportation orbs as well."

"We've only got one pair left," Marrid said.

"Well, bring them."

CHAPTER THREE

Meet

THOUGH THESE LANDS were considered 'civilised' by the druidic council, they weren't farmed and tended to by the city-folk. The townspeople seemed too fearful to move much beyond sight of the roads they cut into the hills or the hamlets they cowered in at night.

But *these* civilised people, these *criminals*, had come quite a bit further than most dared.

The sparse collectives of wild-flowers that grew in the open fields gave Heather directions to Galan and the other thieves. They sat perched atop one of the many green hills, one of the only without a tree or two on it.

It had been a cold night with a light drizzle, why hadn't they sought out cover for their camp-site? Heather shrugged. Though the sun was starting to warm them all now, it would rain again before too long.

Galan sat on a blanket he'd spread out over the long grass, smothering it. For what it was worth — not a lot — the grass was feeling rather indignant. But that wasn't anything new for grass.

An orcish looking man, despite sitting, loomed over the others and seemed slightly more at ease in their surroundings. He frowned at the fire, something clearly troubling him, though no one seemed to care. Strange to see someone with orc blood have a mood other than angry, hungry, or horny. At least, that's what her druidic teachings told her to expect from his kind.

The last one, the elf, was clearly not raised in elven villages, or else the bugs wouldn't bother him so. Perched atop a log with his feet crossed, he alternated between drumming a beat on his legs and swatting away insects. He coughed once in the smoke from the fire and moved to the other end of the log. The smoke followed him. Definitely not a true elf.

What an odd group of outcasts. They were her only option though, so she stepped into their little circle.

"Pack up your things," she said, trying to sound confident. "There's a small bluff we—"

The three men jumped to their feet. Galan produced a knife, though from where she had no idea. The orc was on his feet far faster than she expected his bulk would allow, and the elf had made a daring leap to cross the fire and hide behind the orc. His arms wielded a wooden device with strands of old sheep intestine stretched over it, some kind of weapon?

Dealing with people was such a pain. One of the very few good parts of being a druid was you never really ran into anyone. She wasn't well-versed in whatever social niceties were expected of her.

"I'm sorry," she said. "Let me start again. Hello weary travellers from yonder city. Greetings, Galan, whom I have already met. Do you recall our prior arrangement?"

"What?" The half-orc's voice was like thunder rolling down a mountain. He turned to Galan. "Is that her?"

"Yes." Galan held one hand against his heart and breathed. He flourished his hand at Heather while turning to the other two, the knife was nowhere to be seen. "Allow me to introduce to you, Lady Heatherdown of Farrowood."

This was going much better now. Nature didn't care much for greetings. "Yes. Hello."

"Oh um." Galan hopped onto the elf's log. "Allow me to introduce to you, Grog, the orcish looking fellow. He's really, very good at... well he's very big. And the faint shadow of an elf there is Elvalor, one of—"

The elf shot Galan a look.

"—Sorry. Elvalor is *the* best musician in all of The Three Kingdoms. And he's also quite an orator, capable of convincing the most stoic and duty-driven of guards to hand over the keys to the city."

"I see. And you're all burglars?"

"Ah, no." Galan held a finger up. "We're thieves. Burglars are unnecessarily destructive."

"And I'm not a thief," said Elvalor. "At least, not ordinarily. Unfortunately, music doesn't always pay well."

"I see," Heather said, though she didn't see. "And you?" she asked Grog. What kind of a name was that?

"I'm a thief. Sometimes I dip my toe into a bit of robbery as well."

"Oh, I see, I see." Heather definitely did not see. "Well. As I was saying, there's a bluff a little to the north of here, which would make a much nicer camping spot. It's only an hour's walk. We should get there before the storm."

"Storm?" Galan gazed up at the brightening morning.

The majority of the night's oppressive grey clouds had moved on. "Looks clear to me."

Heather rolled her eyes. She knew city-people would be ignorant of the natural ways, but surely they would know that a druid would have a pretty good inkling of when it was going to rain?

"If we don't get a move on soon you're all going to get very wet," she told them. "We won't make it to what you call Farrowood before it hits."

Elvalor moved his mouth to speak.

Heather cut him off. "You won't make it back to Threerun in time either."

The three of them looked at each other for a moment. A heavy, rain-scented wind whipped up at them from the grass. Although they probably couldn't detect it, the breeze kicked something instinctual in them. They moved about, gathering and packing their things.

Grog made a show of kicking dirt over the fire and fussing the embers around with a stick. Orcs weren't smart, but even *they* wouldn't bother with more than a bit of dirt when a storm was coming.

Despite her constant urging, travel was slow. At one point, as her frustration was beginning to boil over, she stopped and waited for them to trudge past her. Their footfalls were all *wrong*! Instead of stepping between each sprout of grass, they tended to just... well they just *stepped*. There was no care at all to where they put their feet. No wonder grass was always so quick to anger.

They walked in a single file with Heather in the lead. When they were only halfway to shelter, fat drops of rain started to slap against them.

"Is it much farther?" Elvalor asked.

"Yes. It's much further," Heather responded. "We're halfway there." There didn't seem much point in telling them that on her own she would already be there by now.

"So, this unicorn you want us to steal," Grog said. "What's the story there?"

Heather could barely recall any stories from her parents. "I'm sorry, I don't know any unicorn stories."

"What he means is." Galan bounded forward to catch up with her. "How did you know about the unicorn?"

"We have the trees keep an eye on them. They're a protected species, not many of them are left."

"Why's that?" Grog asked.

"Over-hunting," Heather said.

"Ah yes," Elvalor sang out from the back of the column. "Ground unicorn horn is quite the aphrodisiac."

"I've heard that a unicorn horn can bring back the dead," Galan said.

"Is it true," Grog asked. "That only a virgin can catch one?"

"Count Radu is *definitely* not a virgin," Galan declared. "Rich guy like that, with all the black and red velvet trappings of a vampire about."

"He wouldn't have caught it himself," Grog said.

"Wellll," Elvalor said. "Rumour has it that many young women and men who go missing in The Three Kingdoms are actually being lured, or caught depending on who's telling it, to Count Radu. So he can feast on them. Virgin blood is what he craves. Perhaps he used one of them to catch the unicorn?"

What were they talking about? You didn't need to be a virgin to catch a unicorn. Sure, they had a bit of natural magic but they weren't weird about it like some of the *gods* were.

"So you want to free the unicorn," Grog said. "And pay a lot of money to do so?"

"Yes," Heather said. "Is there something wrong?"

"No," Grog rumbled. "Animals should be free. Not a lot of people will pay to make it happen, though."

A flash of distant lightning urged the three of them a little faster. Rivulets ran between the hills, getting faster and wider the longer they travelled. Heather did her best to demonstrate how to cross them, dancing over the stones and logs, but the others trudged through. Elvalor had a good go at it, but slipped and fell. He didn't make another attempt at crossing them her way.

Heather stopped when they reached the bluff and called them back, the idiots had run right past it. It *was* fairly innocuous, a little overhang of dirt and rock, long grass weighed by the rain falling over it, nestled between two hillocks. If the wild-flowers didn't tell her it was here, she very well could have walked right past it too.

The hump of dirt under it was kept dry from the little stream that otherwise flooded the gap. Heather leaned against the earthen wall. Elvalor was soaked to the bone, the other two didn't look much better. None of them were having a good time.

"Do you guys want a fire?" she asked.

"Now that." Galan sprung to his feet. "Is a wonderful idea."

He slung off his backpack and rummaged through it, eventually producing a small piece of flint and a metal loop. Heather said nothing as he grabbed a clump of grass from above, shook the water free of it, and balled it up on the ground.

Grog went through his bag, found a bundle of kindling,

and handed it to Galan. Elvalor watched on with interest and made a few encouraging sounds as Galan began striking sparks at the wet grass.

Were they really this ignorant?

"Do you need some help?" she asked.

"No, no. I've got it," Galan said. "I think we just need a little more loose stuff to get it going."

"Here." Elvalor tore grass from behind him that was at least dry. "Try this."

Galan nodded his thanks, rolled the grass up, stuffed it into his little temple of sticks, and struck the flint some more.

"I'm not sure what the problem is," he said. "It worked so well last time."

Heather had to admire their commitment. She let them take turns, and make suggestions — none of which helped — until she got cold.

"Allow me," she said. "I'm quite practised at this."

After removing everything wet, she pulled two dead strings of grass from the dirt in front of her, and laid them together. On top, she placed a single piece of kindling. The grass caught after her second strike of the flint, quickly licking up the kindling. Galan moved to put the rest of the kindling on top.

"No, don't put that on," she said. "It won't burn for long."

With a wave of her hand, a tree-root grew up out of the ground, dried, and fell to the dirt. She placed it on the fire.

"There, that will burn better," she said.

"That must come in handy." Elvalor's eyes were wide. "I've not seen magic like that before."

Heather wasn't surprised, it was clear he'd never lived with his own kind before. She made an attempt at a smile to acknowledge him but she feared it looked forced. This was the first time she'd sat with so many non-druids since... well since *forever*.

Firelight danced off the little waterfalls that curtained the overhang. Grog pulled out a piece of something from his pack that smelled like mulched reeds, but they'd been flattened into a thin sheet. With it came a small container of liquefied charcoal and the flight feather of a goose. He used the liquid to scrawl markings on the sheet with the needle end of the feather. "Tell me," Grog said after a few minutes. "Where does a druid come up with so many gold coins?"

There it was, she knew the question was coming. From when she was young, learning the druid ways, she'd been warned it was all civilised folk cared for. Money. Money, money, money. She'd need to get some for herself if everything went to plan.

"The elder council provided me with quite a few funds. We take our guardianship of the unicorns very seriously," she said.

Grog studied her face. "Where does a druid keep so many coins?"

"In my bag of course." She patted the old satchel.

"What's to stop us taking those coins, and leaving you for dead?" Grog asked.

Galan didn't react other than to watch her. She thought he'd at least make a half-hearted attempt to settle things down. Elvalor, despite his and her shared racial lineage, did nothing. She wasn't even sure he'd heard the question, as busy as he was checking over the strange sheep intestine contraption he carried. Maybe the druids were right, all these people cared about was money.

With a reluctant sigh, she asked the grass behind the

three of them to grow and twine around their legs. It took a moment for them to realise what was happening. While Galan and Elvalor looked suitably surprised, Grog remained calm and settled his gaze back upon her.

She met his eyes. "The entire natural world is stopping you from..."

His face lit up in fear. It was as plain as it was on a mouse hearing the screech of a diving owl. Elvalor screamed. All three of them struggled against the grass and stared past her.

She jumped and hit her head on the rock above as she turned. Coming over the lip of the overhang, upside-down, was Legs. Shiny and slick from the rain, spindly legs reaching out for purchase. God the thing was horrible.

"Oh fuck," she shuddered. "Do you *always* have to do that you horrid thing? Go away." She pointed off behind it. "Go away and leave me alone. Just. I don't know, sit in a tree out there somewhere."

It came all the way around and cocked its furry head to the side, all eight eyes upon her.

"No. No!" She clapped her hands. "Bad. Go away."

Instead, Legs skittered to the ground and nestled itself in the corner. It probably thought it was camouflaged but was too stupid to know how completely visible it was. So long as it stayed over there, fine.

She turned back to the others, all still struggling against the grass.

"Oh, don't worry," she said. "That's just Legs."

SENTINEL JANU HUNCHED down and poked at the still-warm remains of a fire. Ainsworth bent over, held one hand against the rock of the overhang above, and with the point of his sword, sifted through a mess of grass and spider-webs. Drips of water splashed down from overhead. Outside, Marrid's footsteps squelched back and forth as he mumbled to himself.

"Anything?" Janu asked Ainsworth.

"No, there's just a dead rat here. What about the fire? Anything interesting?"

"It would help if I knew what I was looking for," she said. It didn't matter how many times she pointed it out, Ainsworth's response was always the same. He couldn't tell her anything that might identify the informant, blah blah blah.

"Maybe it would be better if you wait with Marrid. Let *me* find any message from the informant."

The gall! She was his superior. He needed to learn how things *really* worked.

"You are hindering our investigation. *My* investigation. We are here to prevent a crime, a very serious crime."

"Sir, I know. But I can't divulge the informant's name. There are rules in place for a reason."

"The reasons are bullshit," she accused. "Out here, when it comes time to bust heads and make arrests, those rules don't apply. Do you think Galan and Grog play by those rules?"

"Sir..."

Dammit! "Fine. I'll wait for you outside."

After ducking out, she strode up the incline to find Marrid, surrounded by their three backpacks, gazing out to the north. He was, as always, armoured and armed, ready for a fight. A bleak greyness sat over the horizon, leeching the colour from the hills. The overhead clouds still threatened rain and hampered the sun.

"Anything?" she asked.

"No, Janu," Marrid said. "They're long gone by now. Not

that it matters, we know where they're going."

"Yes."

"So why bother following them? If we stayed to the road, we could have taken a wagon up to Kalindar and beat them. This overland travel has got to slow them down."

"Sir!" Ainsworth dashed up the slope toward them. "Our informant has left us some new information. The druid, Lady Heatherdown, appears to be quite powerful. They recommend we have a magic user to help counter her abilities when it comes time for the arrest."

Sentinel Janu summoned her dagger from its sheath at her belt. It floated to her hand. She grasped it and held it up. "I think I've got it covered," she said.

Ainsworth looked pained. "The informant says she has magic over the natural world, sir. A *real* druid, like from the old stories."

"In a different league to your little prestidigitations," Marrid confirmed. "We're going to need a wizard."

"Or a sorcerer," Ainsworth added.

"Alright." Janu pinched the bridge of her nose. "We don't have any mages in the Sentinels. Marrid, who do we usually employ for that sort of thing?"

Marrid scratched the side of his head. "It's been a while."

"Sirs?" Ainsworth interrupted. "I know of a sorcerer in Kalindar. Seeing as we're headed that way... I'm sure she would be of help."

"What's her name?" Janu asked.

"My mother, sir. Gwyn."

Galan wasn't anywhere near as clever as he thought he was, but he was a tenacious bastard. A powerful druid was definitely something out of left field, and Janu didn't for a second believe that this... *unicorn heist* was what it seemed.

No. Druids don't have money, they don't employ thieves to free magical beasts from undead party hosts. There was more to this, and she'd uncover it, and put an end to the Thieves' Guild for good.

"Alright," Janu said. "Ainsworth, head west until you get to the King's trail and go to Kalindar. There should be plenty of guard patrols you can hitch a ride with. We'll keep following the thieves, just tell me how to spot the informant's messages."

"Sir...," Ainsworth said. "You know I ca—"

"—I'm not asking for a name." Janu held her hand up. "Just how to spot the messages so we can follow them."

Ainsworth studied his feet. He stayed that way for a few seconds, almost long enough for Janu to tell him she'd changed her mind.

"Okay," he said. "You just need to look for a cross. It could be a mark, or two overlapping branches. The easier it is to find where they've been, like here where they had a fire, the smaller the cross. This one was just two twigs."

It was hardly the revelation she was hoping for, and there was no way she could ascertain an identity with it. Did Ainsworth actually know who it was?

"The last message said they're heading north, through the forest, before they cut west to cross the mountains."

What was Galan doing? Crossing the mountains from the west to reach Kalindar was needless. The trails down here in the south led almost straight to the north, through the pass into the capital's valley. Going out of your way to trek through the forest, and then hike over a mountain... he was up to something.

"Get a move on, Ainsworth," she ordered. "When you get to Kalindar, keep a low profile. Don't announce yourself to the Sentinels there, but if you need to, work with the city guards. They'll be happy to work under the Sentinel's noses. Come on Marrid, we've got some time to make up now."

"Here, take this." Marrid handed Ainsworth one of the teleportation orbs. "You've got the receiving end, so if you run into trouble, just twist and drop it."

Ainsworth nodded, took his pack and departed.

Galan was a slippery one. There was once a time when Janu knew all the tricks of the trade, but it had been a lifetime since she'd escaped the underbelly. Too many of her old skills were lost. But it didn't matter. Whatever Galan was up to, she'd put a stop to it.

IT WAS COLD, damp, and Galan had had enough of all this walking. At first the hills, with their water-heavy, waist-high grass were endless. But they did end. It was the *forest* that had no end, just mile after mile of sodden logs to clamber over, and clouds of incessant, swarming insects. He wasn't sure he had any more blood for them to drain, and was adamant he had run out of sweat a day ago.

Damn he was thirsty. He lifted his waterskin and gave it a shake over his open mouth. Not even a drop. You would think with all the rain still dripping down through the trees they'd have come across a stream or something by now. It wasn't time to ask the druid for help yet, he'd save that for later.

Pausing under a pine, he tilted his head back to capture some of the drips. Something big and black moved along the branch above him.

"Gah! Fuck!"

He couldn't help it. Every time he caught sight of Legs it gave him the same reaction. Who the hell has a giant spider as a pet? Who even knew such things existed?

"Does it always have to sit above me?" he called out to Lady Heatherdown.

"Yeah. He does that," she said. "Sorry."

She was walking out in front of Elvalor and Grog, stepping through the dense underbrush with apparent ease. Grog, Elvalor, and Galan tried to keep up with her but it was clear they were slowing her down. Still... this was *his* job, they were supposed to be moving at *his* pace. She may be the benefactor, and far more adept at travelling through the countryside, but he was in charge.

"Let's stop for lunch." Galan used the commanding tone he'd perfected over the years in the guild.

"It's not lunch time," Heatherdown called back. "And we had a break only two hours ago."

Elvalor and Grog stopped between the two leaders, looking first at one and then the other. Grog raised an eyebrow.

This wasn't right. Galan lowered his voice. "We will stop for a fifteen minute break. We could use a rest."

The others didn't need any more convincing, but Heatherdown scowled and paused before coming back and joining them. Galan checked the surrounding trees for any sign of Legs but found none. Creepy fucking thing.

He sat on a log and frowned at the dampness immediately seeping through his trousers. "Where's your spider? Out making a web?"

"What?" Her brow creased in confusion. "No. He's too stupid to make a web." She stood slightly apart from them, unwilling to let them rest for long.

"Actually." Grog lowered himself onto a stone. "I don't think it's a web-spinning spider. Looks more like a hunter to me."

"No," Heatherdown declared. "He's just stupid. I don't even know why it hangs around. I wish it would go away." She paced around them.

"Can't you, like..." Elvalor looked up. "Can't you *make* it? With your nature magic?"

She sighed and slumped her shoulders. A small branch held her attention. "No. He's my *animal companion*. I can't get rid of him. It's like... a symbol of my closeness to nature, we have a bond."

"A bond?" Grog chewed on what appeared to be a piece of dried meat. Galan had finished all his a while ago, he asked Grog this morning but his friend swore he had none left.

"Yeah, a bond, a magical bond," Heatherdown said. "I'm supposed to be able to communicate with him and see what he sees. But it doesn't work, he's too stupid."

"Is it true you can transform into an animal?" Grog asked.

"Well... yes. But it's not something that's done."

Grog tugged on the dried meat. "Aren't you able to?"

She averted her eyes and remained silent. That was more like it. So long as she announced doubts about her abilities, it would be a lot easier for Galan to keep everything under control. It was time to discuss plans.

"So," Galan said, bringing everyone's attention back to himself. "You might be wondering why Lady Heatherdown has taken us off-road and into the forest."

"I had wondered," Elvalor said. "We could have travelled to Kalindar by now if we'd only stayed on the King's trail. I figured you wanted to remain unnoticed."

"We're here to pick up the last member of our crew." Galan didn't miss the confused look from Lady

Heatherdown. She really did think she was in charge of things. "She's crossing through the forest from Northend."

"Who?" Grog asked.

There was a time, not so long ago, when Grog wouldn't ask any questions. He used to trust Galan's judgement completely. But now that trust was down to a single, sinuous strand. Just enough to get Grog out on this one last heist. At least when it was done, Galan would know that he did everything he could for his best friend, even if they wouldn't be guild-mates anymore.

Galan cleared his throat. "A dwarf named Jendora."

"What do we need with a dwarf?" Heatherdown asked.

"Tell me, Lady Heatherdown." Galan turned to regard her. "How did you plan for us to leave the castle with the unicorn?"

"Well, I." She frowned. "I hired you to figure that out."

"Yes," Galan agreed. "Jendora is a caver. She'll lead us out through the catacombs into The End."

"What!" Grog and Elvalor leapt to their feet in unison.

"We'll die there," Elvalor said.

"Galan." Grog held his arms wide. "You can't be serious? We'll starve or die of thirst before we find somewhere to cross back over the mountains. My bag of holding only carries so much."

"Or we'll get eaten by a Purple Worm!" Elvalor cried.

Much the reaction he'd expected. Everyone knew the desert on the other side of the northern mountains — The End — couldn't be travelled. It was the source of every evil creature that threatened a village of good people, every bad omen, every wayward decision. Hogwash.

"No. We won't," Galan said simply. "Lady Heatherdown? I'm thirsty, would you mind filling my waterskin?" He held the empty skin up and gave it a little shake.

With a deepening frown, she waved a hand at it. It grew fat and heavy, condensation beaded on the outside. Galan wobbled it, letting water slosh out the top.

"Sometimes, Galan," Elvalor said. "You come up with some really good ideas."

"Thank you." Galan smiled. "We'll head west in The End, skirting the edges of the mountains, and cross back to the south at Northend. Farrowood is just east of there. As far as the Sentinels will be concerned, whoever made off with the unicorn will have vanished." He flashed his hands and slowly parted them.

"Everyone is paid and we can all be on our merry way?" Grog asked.

That stung. Was Grog planning on not returning to Threerun at least? Galan had thought Grog would bring his family out and stay nearby where they could visit each other and reminisce. He forced a smile onto his face. "Jendora shouldn't be long, she said she wouldn't have any trouble tracking us down here."

"Isn't a dwarf tracking you in a forest a little odd?" Heatherdown made it sound like an accusation.

"No, no. That's what she does. Hunts people. Ah! Here she is now."

CHAPTER FOUR

Tunnels

HEATHER HUNG BACK from the others as they approached the edge of the forest. Rain clouds tore across the jagged, grey mountains looming in the near distance. The day had grown darker ever since Jendora had caught up with them, and looked to be getting worse. There was no doubt it would rain before they got to Kalindar, and those mountains were treacherous on a good day.

"We should probably camp here the night," Heather called out. "There's a series of very large logs a little way north we can camp in and stay out of the rain."

"It's alright," Jendora replied. "It won't rain where we're going."

Jendora pulled her thick cloak tight around her shoulders. Though Heather had never before met a dwarf, she had learned a lot about them from the trees and rocks. Of course, she couldn't really speak to the rocks, but the trees could, so they interpreted for her. There must have been something lost in translation though, because Jendora didn't wear any metal armour and didn't have a beard. In fact, the only metal she carried was the roped hooks sitting in loops on her belt. Everything else was hide or leather, well-kept and well-used. Although several beasts had to die to produce her clothing, she appeared to respect what the creatures' death gave her.

According to Heather's parents, there were fewer things worse than a dwarf. Despite her lifelong suspicion that a certain amount of racism may have been involved, this dwarf did very little to convince Heather otherwise. It was going to rain. Hard. And those mountains would be a mess of water and mud in no time.

"It will rain." Though Heather was losing patience with these people, she did her best to keep her tone neutral. The look from Elvalor probably meant it wasn't working. "I mean to say, I believe that it will rain soon, and it will rain on the mountains so we shouldn't try a crossing just yet. I am a druid, you know? I know about these sorts of things."

"There's no time," Galan called out.

His insistence to be the one in charge reminded her of a queen bee. Although it wouldn't interfere with her plans, it still annoyed her. He was lucky Count Radu's party was the most definite way to gain access to his mansion. If that ever changed she would abandon these people and find another thief to sneak her in.

"Kalindar is a day away at best," Heather said. "There's no need to press on now. We can wait for the storm to pass and cross the mountain tomorrow."

Jendora laughed, a light fluttering sound, not unlike birdsong. "You keeping all your plans to yourself like usual, Galan?"

The corner of Galan's mouth curved up, ever so slightly,

but he managed to suppress the smile. "Old habits die hard." He looked at Heather and gave a shrug as he walked. "I'm sorry. We're going *under* the mountain. Jendora will be our guide. Much easier than traipsing over the top in all the rain."

"No rain underground." Grog nodded sagely.

Was it normal for hired professionals to do their own thing without checking? The druidic council was no doubt a little out of touch with culture and society, but they were adamant the plan would work. Now here the thieves were, coming up with their own plans. She needed to keep on top of things. Galan's insistence to be in charge made a lot more sense now, it was the only way to ensure everyone did what you wanted.

Fine.

"Okay, thanks. That's a good idea, Jendora. I'm glad to have you on my team." Heather kept her eyes on Galan as she spoke. He gave no reaction. "My people speak highly of the mountain homes. I hope one day to visit them."

Elvalor leaned in close and whispered. "Probably best not to mention 'home'. She's an exile."

Jendora spat. "They're fucked," she said. "They're going to war with the elves."

"Oh." Heather didn't even know they did that sort of thing. War wasn't very natural. "What did you do to be exiled?"

In a whirl of cloak and ropes, Jendora appeared directly in front of her, hardened eyes glaring. In one hand, she held the front of Heather's clothes, in the other, one of the hooks. How had she moved so quickly?

"I didn't do a fucking thing," Jendora said in a voice just for Heather. "Not a fucking thing. Do you understand?"

Heather could only nod. What was wrong with these people?

Jendora released her and moved to the front of their marching column. She said a few words to Galan that Heather couldn't hear, then stepped into the lead. Everyone continued on.

Without the trees and underbrush as a barrier, the wind whipped at the group's clothes and stirred the grass, sprinkling them all in a fine water mist. Waves of rolling thunder passed over them, felt in the gut more than heard. From all around came the fear and panic of the mice, rabbits, and other little creatures, scurrying away into their burrows of safety. Heather did her best to push those feelings away and shield herself, but nature was never far away.

Jendora stopped and pointed at a gap in the base of a hill.

"Down here," she said. "It's a bit slippery, so just slide in. I'll go first. Don't make me wait."

Then she was gone. Head first into a hole in the ground.

Galan leapt to the mound above the hole. He kicked a few fallen branches to the side and crossed his arms. "Alright, you heard her. Let's get a move on."

"Hold on a second, Galan." Elvalor held his palm up. "Who's this dwarf? How many more splits of the loot are we going to have?"

"Enough of that," Galan replied. "You'll be earning more on this job than in a year of caterwauling."

"No, no." Elvalor's demeanour had changed, so abruptly Heather was sure it wasn't him. "Listen to me. *Her* cut is coming from *your* pay. *Not* from mine. Understand?"

When she'd first met them, Heather thought Elvalor was harmless, nothing more than a tool Galan was using to gain access to the castle. But not anymore. Now he waved a branch — that he'd been using to hike — with a vague threat of violence. Animals were so much simpler than people.

"Do you have any idea who you're talking to?" Galan glowered down from his position above the hole. "I am the leader of the Thieves' Guild. You should count yourself lucky that you've even been hired."

"There ain't no guild anymore and everyone knows it," Elvalor said.

"Is that right?" Galan nodded to Grog. "Well, out here there's a guild, and you're right in the middle of it."

Grog stepped his feet apart and folded his arms.

"Rough him up a little, Grog." Galan flicked a hand toward Elvalor. "Teach him a lesson."

Grog didn't move and didn't speak.

Elvalor watched him from the corner of his eye. "I think maybe you're a bit out of sort there, Galan. Like I said. It comes out of your cut."

He snapped his hiking branch over his knee and tossed the two parts to the ground. Then, like Jendora, Elvalor was gone.

Galan's face remained emotionless as he stared at Grog. Grog remained silent and stared back. With a quick smirk, Galan dropped down into the hole.

"That had been coming for a long time," Grog said to Heather. "I hope for your sake, you've got the coin you promised. You better go."

Heather took his advice and slid into the hole. This whole thing might have been a mistake.

DESPITE THE RAIN outside and the smell of damp air, the cave was dry. With all the moisture above ground, Janu knew to expect an underground river once they got further in. For now, everything sparkled and glinted in the sunlight streaming through the entry hole, but darkness killed off the starry patterns after only a few metres.

If the informant hadn't left the crossed branches, they never would have known the thieves had gone underground. Though the sticks were stuck upright in the grass, she and Marrid were very lucky to have come across them. Tracking people through the wilderness was a lot different than tracking them through the city. Good thing Marrid had a bit of skill at it, though how a dwarf learned to track people above ground wasn't a secret he was willing to share.

Janu leaned around a stalagmite then ducked back behind it. Something moved up ahead, she was sure of it. Behind her, in the last remnants of sunlight, Marrid hunched behind a limestone deposit. He raised an eyebrow and mouthed a silent question. Again, in the cave ahead, a darker shadow flitted across the brown-grey space between the columns of stone. There was definitely something down there.

Wasn't there?

Without light, the stone seemed to absorb the darkness around it, leaving no distinction of its shape, no way to discern what was air versus rock. Only faint drips interspersed by silence reached her ears. She ground her teeth in frustration. Marrid's suggestion he go first with his dwarven eyes was right. She couldn't see shit down here.

She beckoned him over.

"What is it?" he whispered. "Do you see something?"

Was this his attempt at questioning her decisions? "I need you to go ahead," she whispered back. "Keep an eye out."

With a short nod, Marrid continued in his crouch,

battleaxe prepared to strike. Despite the bulk of his armour, he moved with soft, sure steps, and in complete silence. Imagine being snuck up on by a fully armoured dwarf... it must have taken him many years of training. Conventional wisdom told her that dwarven tactics required shock troops and martial prowess. How many other denizens of the mountain homes could move like he did, could track prey through a forest?

Staying directly behind Marrid, Janu found she could follow him by keeping the darkest blob in the centre of her vision. At least that was the idea. She bumped into his back.

Marrid cursed in Dwarven. "This isn't working," he whispered, a little too loudly. "You can't see in the dark as I do. You're no svirfneblin. Light a lantern at the least."

He was right, but damn it, she didn't want to risk alerting the thieves to their presence. It was easy to stay unnoticed above ground, surrounded by hills or forests, but not so much down here when shining a beacon ahead of you.

"How far behind them do you think we are?" she asked.

She could feel Marrid frown even without seeing his face. "Hard to say. If you're worried about being detected, let me go ahead. If I see something, I'll come back and warn you before they ever see the light."

That was a solid plan. From her backpack she removed a simple lantern — taken from the Sentinel depot — and lit it with a small flint contraption that sparked and flashed light through the cave when activated. With the wick caught, she turned the valve until the flame struggled to hold its form, then turned it down even more. It flickered weakly but stayed alight.

On the ground in front of them, a small pile of stones had been arranged in a cross, a handy confirmation they were going the right way.

Marrid saw the stones and spoke in a harsh whisper. "Wait a minute or two, then follow. If there are any branching paths, wait for me to return."

Janu nodded, there was no option but to rely on Marrid's eyes. She was used to watching and stalking in the shadows, but hills and caverns were very different to streets and warehouses. Her people abandoned their semi-underground village when she was only an infant, nothing but cloudy memories of the scant light and scent of earth remained. Working in an underground office was one thing, but she had to admit, she wasn't much of a gnome anymore.

She'd need to lean on Marrid down here. He was a good dwarf, a good Sentinel, even if he wasn't officially one. If she was forced to be dependent on someone, she could do worse than Marrid... still, she shifted uncomfortably with the thought.

"Remember to keep an eye behind you as well," Marrid said. "Down here, things have a habit of sneaking up to your back."

She sat the lantern on the ground and kept her eyes moving. Light glistened back from a hundred different places. The striated patterns in the stone kindled a childhood memory from a teacher long dead. This rock had come from deep, very deep, formed aeons before gnomes, dwarves, or really *anyone* had lived. The ever-present movements of the mountains and valleys had pushed it up, over a million years, to where it was now. Was it still connected to the core? Had it brought with it the unspeakable horrors that dwelt within?

It's just the dark, and she was a Sentinel, damn it. Living in fear was behind her. This was nothing compared to life as an orphan in the alleys of Threerun.

She rolled up her sleeves and loosened her hands.

The hairs on the back of her arms stood up. That feeling had saved her life once before, when a bandit aimed a crossbow at her from a second story balcony. As she did then, she dove forward, onto her side and looked up. But unlike back then, a clunky backpack hampered her movement, so she caught only a glimpse of whatever it was that skittered along the ceiling.

It had been black, and bulbous, with curved legs that melted into the dark rock around it. If she didn't know any better, she would swear it was a spider. Had Galan led her into a subterranean spider den? A sneaking suspicion this was all planned crept up the back of her mind, but she forced it down. No. If Galan had done so, it was by accident, there was no plan.

Janu got to her feet, scooped up the lantern, and drew her sword. Why didn't she already have it at the ready like Marrid? She wasted no time and moved further into the cave. Whether it was a spider or something more sinister didn't matter, the more blades that faced an adversary the better. A lesson learned long before she became a Sentinel.

Something hooked into the fabric of her trouser and yanked. She fell forward, losing her light and only just managing to not break her nose. Instinct bade her to roll and face the threat, but the weight of the backpack, and something else, held her down.

Three loud clanks echoed in the narrow space and she was suddenly freed. Leaping to her feet, she shrugged off the pack, gripped her sword with both hands, and pulled it back for a strike.

The sight of Marrid stopped her mid-swing. His eyes

quivered with concern, bordering on fear, something she never thought she'd see.

"Spider," he said. "I don't know where it went."

He turned his back to her and she did the same to him. There were two of them now, and two sets of eyes meant one less direction to sneak up on. Her eyes darted to the ceiling, but there was nothing.

They stayed that way for some time before she spoke.

"We need to keep moving, we can't lose Galan."

With a grunt of agreement, Marrid led the way. Janu walked backwards a lot of the time, readying herself against every flicker of shadow cast by the lantern. They travelled for what she guessed was a few hours, but tired feet and darkness made it hard to gauge the passage of time.

Water slicked across the path in a few areas, slimy sheets of it running down one wall and disappearing at the base of another. Marrid slowed his pace and took careful steps across the wet rocks. Janu took his lead and did the same.

A larger section of cave with a split path brought them to an uncertain stop. Janu waited for Marrid to listen down each tunnel, and did the same herself, but there was nothing except the occasional trickle of water. There was no sign of a cross.

Marrid stuck his head down both pathways a second time. "I think they've gone this way." He pointed down the left path. "Wait here."

Had he forgotten who was in charge? "What makes you so sure?"

"There's a faint pull on the air. The other tunnel doesn't have it. I'm guessing this one starts heading up into the Kalindar valley, and the other one..."

"...the other one what?"

"It goes down. They wouldn't have gone that way."

"Alright. Lead the way."

Before they had made it ten metres down the tunnel, Janu stepped in something soft and spongy. It looked like a leathery skin, the last remnants of some fallen creature. As she lifted her boot it clung to her, rising and splitting, until it snapped back to its wet pile. Moistness glossed over the surface of it.

"What is it?" she asked. Her body shuddered.

She wasn't expecting an answer, but Marrid offered one anyway. "We don't want to hang around and find out."

Further on, the tunnel opened up into a large cavern. Three natural pillars of rock stood in the centre of the space, all dripping with moisture, scattering her lantern's light along every surface. Across the floor, a shallow indent in the stone ran from one end of the cave to the other, filled with dark, flowing water. The walls, ceiling, and even the floor were covered in craters of every size, the depths of which remained obscured in shadow.

The last remnants of a light faded down a tunnel on the other side of the cavern.

"There they are," she said. "Just up ahead."

Marrid stepped forward, battleaxe ready.

"Hold on." Janu grabbed him by the bicep. "They haven't done anything yet. We're just following them, hopefully find out what they're up to."

They waited in silence for a few minutes, then Janu rose. "Let's go," she said.

Marrid took the lead again, skirting the edge of her vision. A scraping sound behind them pulled Janu around, sword thrust out in a defensive pose, but nothing was there. Was it her own footfall echoed back?

When she turned back, Marrid came down the tunnel.

"Close the lantern," he said. "They're up ahead."

By holding onto his belt, Janu could walk without bumping into any walls or outcroppings. A pin-prick of light bobbed in the utter black that encased them. They stopped.

"There they are," Marrid said. "Do you see the lantern?"

The light was so small. "Yes," Janu said. "How far away are they?"

"They are on the other side of the chasm. There's a route along the wall to our left that goes all the way around. But they've stopped."

No matter how long she waited, her eyes couldn't adjust to this darkness. "I can't see anything. Is it safe to light the lantern?"

"No. They'll see."

Janu turned her ear to face the light. "Can you hear them?"

"No... wait."

There it was, the thieves were talking and getting more agitated, their voices rising and carrying.

"Don't fucking touch me. Do you understand?" an angry woman's voice said.

"I didn't touch you. I swear it," a male voice said.

"Elvalor." The rumble of Grog was unmistakable. "Don't mess with us."

"I'm not," the male voice insisted. "Hey!"

Galan spoke over them all. "Something just brushed past me."

A woman screamed. The pin-prick of light started swinging. A sudden burst of flames lit up the cavern, revealing a woman suspended halfway to the ceiling, a sinuous rope wrapped around her head.

Grog grabbed the woman and held her as Galan flicked flashes of steel into the space above them. A mound of fleshy wetness screeched as it fell to the ground, the tentacle going slack and falling over Grog's shoulder. The woman unwound the thing from around her neck as Grog put her feet back to the floor.

"What the fuck!" she said.

"Calscarn!" the angry woman, a dwarf, shouted and slammed a hook into the thing on the ground.

Marrid gasped.

As the dwarf woman's voice reverberated around the cavern, several more tentacles lowered from the ceiling. She swung a hooked rope around her head and lashed it up, but tentacles caught and tangled with it before it struck. She set her feet and pulled, but slipped across the ground toward their grasping reach.

The other woman stepped away from Grog and pressed a palm toward the flames burning on the stone. They grew in intensity as another tentacle wrapped itself around her outstretched arm. She yelped and dragged what looked like a branch along the length of flesh that gripped her, splitting the thing into a long blossom of bright blood.

"They need help," Marrid said. "They don't know how to fight Calscarn. You need to hit the head."

A new scream drew Janu's attention back to the thieves. Galan and Grog were ensnared now, only an elf, looking frantically for an exit, remained unaccosted.

"Let's go." She pushed past Marrid and headed toward the path around the chasm's edge.

It was barely wide enough for her to step, with an outcropping of rock that threatened to push her off if she wasn't careful. But she ran anyway, hoping her speed alone would be enough to span the distance.

She yelled as her feet landed on the opposite platform, and made straight for Galan. He had to live, he had to continue on with his robbery if she was to arrest them. She grabbed him by the head, jerked it down, and hacked at the tentacle. On the third strike the sword chopped through, eliciting an animalistic screech from above.

"Janu!" Galan smirked through ragged breaths. "What are you doing here?"

"Shut up!" she said.

Marrid ran past, stepped up Grog's bended knee, and thrust a free arm up into the sprawl of tentacles suspended above. They reacted with alarming speed, twirling around his body and reeling him in.

"Pull me down!" Marrid yelled to Grog.

Yanking with his whole torso, Grog gripped and pulled Marrid to the ground, along with three calscarn. Without extricating himself from their tentacles, Marrid used his axe arm to crack the centre of each creature.

The dwarf woman appeared beside Janu, flinging a rope up into the ceiling. She pulled it down, a calscarn attached to the hooked end. Marrid crunched his battleaxe into it as well.

"Jendora!" he said.

Without a second of hesitation, the dwarf woman punched Marrid in the face, sending him sprawling perilously close to the chasm.

"We need to go!" she announced. "There will be more."

A hoop of rope passed over Janu's eyes, and before she could react, it went tight, binding her arms to her sides. The elf kicked Janu's feet out from under her.

"Let's get the fuck out of here," he said.

Janu watched the thieves leave, ignoring the tentacles

that quested down from the ceiling around her. Galan reappeared, glanced above her and then met her eyes. With a shrug, he tossed a knife to her, turned, and ran.

On the ground, with her hands confined to her sides, Janu kicked herself over the knife. With a wiggle of her fingers it floated up into her hand. She sawed the blade through the rope and sprang to her feet, swiping at the calscarn that reached down for her.

With one hand on the back of Marrid's armour, and the other slashing at tentacles, she made her way down the tunnel, following Galan's trail. The circle of fire must have been magical, it still burned despite a lack of wood under it, but its light was fading. A few slaps across Marrid's cheeks woke him.

"We've got no light, and our packs are in there with the calscarn," she told him. "You need to get up and lead us out of here."

Marrid gripped his battleaxe, Janu gripped his belt, and they jogged up the tunnel. She hadn't felt this dependent on others since she was by herself on the streets of Threerun.

"It's going to be a while until we make it out," Marrid said. "We should pace ourselves."

"You're right," she said. "Plus, I don't want to catch up with Galan again. If he thinks we're dead down here, we might be able to surprise them later."

CHAPTER FIVE

Kalindar

Despite the heavy overcast and torrential rain, the comparative starkness of the day blinded Galan as they burst from the cave. As they ran, he rubbed at his eyes to clear them. In the distance he could just make out the hazy silhouette of Kalindar City, the capital of Kalindar Kingdom, its grey stone making it almost indistinguishable from the surrounding mountains it was carved from.

At this altitude, the northern mountains were a desolate place. There were no farms here, no villages. Just the castle nestled between the razor-like mountains, and a river that burst from under its walls. Galan had heard more than a few merchants talk about the run to the castle, how though it was safe from brigands it was hard on the horses, and you'd break an axle to get there. But the profit made it worthwhile, even for something as simple as grain.

He slowed and came to a stop a little way down the hillside, bent over with his hands on his knees. Though he'd always thought himself quick, it had been a while since he'd had to run from the Sentinels. That was usually left to lower-tier members of the guild.

Grog came to a stop next to him and looked back up to the cave. "Do you think they're chasing us?"

"No," Galan said. "Janu is smarter than that. She'll want us to commit a crime before she tries to nab us."

"The fuck do those Sentinels always know what we're up to?" Elvalor asked between panting breaths.

"Sentinels?" Jendora didn't seem to be breathing heavily at all. "Who and what are Sentinels?"

Galan tried to catch a glimpse of Jendora's expression, but she faced away from him. Was it intentional? Was she worried he'd see something? She knew the dwarf that was with Janu, or at least *he* had known Jendora. What was she keeping from them?

"Law enforcement," Grog told her.

Everyone was silent for a moment.

"How did they track us?" Lady Heatherdown asked. "Are they going to be a problem?"

Galan had forgotten about her for a moment, he was sure a second ago she wasn't there.

"No, no." Galan used his most reassuring voice, the one he often used to quell the fears in lower-ranked guild members being sent to rob an arms dealer or wizard. "The Sentinels need to see us commit a crime, or otherwise have evidence, before they can do anything."

"They're supposed to, anyway," Grog added. "Janu doesn't always care."

"Humph." Jendora nodded and kept an eye on the cave up the hill while she checked her hooks and ropes.

Galan gave Lady Heatherdown an apologetic look. "Everything is under control. Their presence is to be expected."

Though Heatherdown didn't seem convinced, she didn't say anything more about it. Galan found reading the druid almost impossible. A lifetime in the forest probably caused her all sorts of social deficiencies... she could make a good thief actually. This attempt at liberating the unicorn proved she had a concept of ownership, so there was definitely a limit to her ethics.

"But how did they track us?" Lady Heatherdown asked again. "I've requested of the grasses and trees, very politely, to cover your tracks. Even a fellow druid would have had a hard time following us down that cave."

"We have an informant," Elvalor announced.

If there was an informant in their midst, and the Sentinels followed them from Threerun, it would have to be Elvalor. Galan certainly wasn't working with the Sentinels, and there was no way Grog was. The druid didn't even know what a Sentinel was, and besides it was her job.

"Are you an informant?" Galan asked Elvalor. "Seems strange how we've been followed since recruiting you into this caper."

"Fuck off, Galan." Elvalor rested a hand on his dagger.

Jendora took two steps away from everyone and readied one of her hooks.

"Hold on, hold on," Grog said. "Let's not be too hasty. We know Janu has got it in for the guild, she always has—"

"—That's right," Galan said. "You wouldn't believe the size of the bribes she's turned away."

"So?" Jendora raised an eyebrow.

"So," Grog continued. "I wouldn't put it past her to have a wizard scry us."

"That's illegal," Elvalor said. "She can't do that without

approval from the city council."

"Maybe not," Galan said. "But it's the most likely scenario. There was always going to be a watchful Sentinel eye on Count Radu's party. This works in our favour though, we know who to look out for."

Nobody spoke. It *was* the most likely scenario, and it's not like Janu was above breaking the rules when it suited her. And there hadn't been an informant in the guild for years. But still…

"Right, well." Galan clapped his hands again. "Let's get a move on, we're only an hour from a warm hearth and a hot meal." He glanced back at Lady Heatherdown as he strode toward the castle. "Can you do anything about this rain?"

DURING A DRUID'S training, they are told a great many things about the natural world. About how wonderful it is, about how *true* and *right* it is. Nothing is more pure, more honest, more *beautiful* than a forest, or a desert, or two dogs fucking.

But the druidic student is also taught about the civilised world. About how debased it is, how it twists the natural order and thumbs its nose at the cycle of birth, growth, and death. Nothing is more corrupted, more tainted than a house, a hamlet, or planned reproduction.

Heather had always thought there was a bit too much desperation in the way the instructors taught these lessons. They repeated the same phrases over and over again, as though by rote. If any of them had ever seen something as marvellous as a castle, they would never have said the things they did.

Kalindar castle dominated the valley. Even the surrounding mountains seemed only to serve as a frame in which to encompass the stone walls and many spires.

Nothing about it was understated. Turrets and towers reached into the sky. Courtyards with manicured gardens surrounded it and filled every available space.

The central building and its associated lawns were wrapped tightly by an imposing, ivy-covered stone wall. Outside this inner wall, an array of smaller stone buildings stood like subjects beneath the royal seat. Each was more illustrious than any building she'd seen in Threerun, but none of them dared to aspire to the greatness of the castle. One of those lesser buildings must be the home of Count Radu.

Another wall ringed these secondary buildings in a not-quite perfect circle. It was the space between this second inner wall and the final outer wall that Kalindar city occupied. From Heather's vantage point on the bluff, she could see ten thousand or more people going about their business. They reminded her so very much of a colony of insects, each one performing its tasks for the betterment of the hive.

How could anyone think something so wondrous was *wrong*? Civilised people were nothing more than social animals when you got right down to it. This castle, the keep, and surrounding town confirmed what she knew to be true.

The druidic council was wrong.

"What? You never seen a castle before?" Jendora shouldered past, on her way to the slope leading down.

"No," Heather said. "I haven't. And if you touch me again I'll leave you dead on this hillside."

"Well." Galan held an arm in front of them and moved them on. "This is probably the only castle you'll see. I think the others are all just ruins now. Lot of money needed to keep a castle running."

Heather gazed at the city and its castle for a moment more before rushing to join the others.

"Why then does this castle remain," she asked Galan. "When all the others are in ruins?"

He cocked his head to the side and shrugged. "It's the capital. The Queen and her throne are here."

"I see," Heather said, though once again she really didn't understand. She knew the Queen of Kalindar was very unlike a queen bee, or ant; but that was all she knew. The druidic council believed this Queen ruled over the other people, but Heather's experience had so far told her no one ruled over these people. Everyone just did what they liked.

That must be a good feeling. Being free to do whatever you wanted, whenever you wanted. Civilisation was a lot more like the natural world than the druids wanted to accept. She wouldn't waste time trying to convince them otherwise, she'd get out soon, and live a full life of luxury. If everything went to plan.

"We'd best go around to the trail and come at the city that way," Elvalor said, pointing to the south. "We don't want an overeager young guard with a good aim to try and protect her majesty too hard."

As they skirted the walls at a distance, the immensity of them took full form. There was no animal that could penetrate these walls, and very few that would comfortably scale them. The massive blocks of stone were so tightly packed that they appeared as a solid slab, surely it wasn't made of bedrock? Heather wanted to rush forward and run her hand along it to be sure.

"It's such a depressing place." Grog wasn't gazing at the castle. He was instead surveying the valley. "Nothing but dirt and pebbles and brown and grey."

"Dead. Lifeless." Galan shook his head.

Heather lowered her mental barrier and allowed the natural world to seep into her mind. Lifeless? This place was teeming. It may not have been full of verdant farmlands and forests, but the soil here carried all manner of insects and burrowing rodents. A snake worked its way under loose soil only ten metres from their path. No less than seventeen lizards were nestled in various rocks nearby, awaiting the sun's re-emergence.

Was there any point in correcting them?

"There's plenty of creepy-crawlies around here," Jendora corrected them. "You can't see them, but they're here. Just because the ground's no good for tilling doesn't mean it's barren."

"Here we are." Galan moved toward the castle to intercept the road.

Twenty trees, old ones at that, must have been felled to create the city's gates. They stood as tall as the walls and almost as thick. Judging by the dirt and dust piled up around their bottoms, they had been left wide open for many years.

"These haven't been moved in a long time," Heather said as they approached.

Galan glanced at her over his shoulder. "No. A thousand years of peace generally keeps city gates open."

It seemed every new snippet of information on the outside world contradicted some axiom of the druidic way of thinking. These people weren't warmongering or unnaturally violent and destructive. Though they built great works such as this, it was no different than a beehive or a termite mound if you thought about it with more than your existing prejudice. It consolidated that she was doing the right thing.

The lone guard at the gate offered them a half-hearted wave as they entered. Within the walls, the city looked the same as Threerun, probably the same as all cities looked. But there *was* a sense of the unnatural here, everything was too ordered, too straight-lined. Whereas Threerun's streets bent to the will of the land it was built on, the ground beneath Kalindar had been carved and beaten into submission.

A flicker of doubt, maybe the council was right, passed across Heather's thoughts. But she ignored it and let it fall away.

"Right." Galan clapped his hands and turned to face the group.

Everyone came to a stop in a semi-circle around him.

"First things first, we'll need lodgings. Grog, you handle that. We're also going to—"

"—hold on, Galan." Grog held a palm out. "I ain't got no money. Can't rent a room." He passed his gaze over the group, coming to a stop on Jendora and Heather. "*Rooms* without any coin."

"I'm sure our financier can put up the money." Elvalor turned to face Heather. "Right?"

"I what?" she asked.

Elvalor rolled his eyes. "Pay for a couple rooms for the next few days."

"Why?"

He scoffed. "Well, because you've got the money."

"I haven't got any money."

Everyone's eyes shot straight to her. Grog took a step toward her.

"What?" Galan crossed his arms. "No money?"

Oh shit! That's right. "Well, I mean, I don't have any money. Just those coin... things... that you're all so fond of."

Would they believe that?

"Yes, yes," Elvalor held his hand out. "Just give me some of them. That's *money*."

Heather breathed a mental sigh of relief. "No. I don't think I will." She put her hands on her hips and set her feet apart, mimicking the stance she'd seen Galan take every time he was asserting himself. "I'll organise the rooms, thank you."

"Fine." Galan pinched the bridge of his nose and waved his hand at Elvalor. "Lady Heatherdown, please find us somewhere to stay. Grog, go with her, make sure nothing happens to her."

"What about the rest of us?" Jendora asked.

"The party's only a few days away. Let's have a look around, map out escape routes, note the guard patrols and all that."

Without further discussion, Galan, Elvalor, and Jendora went down the street to the left. Grog remained where he was. He lifted his chin and watched her, waiting until the others were well out of earshot before he spoke.

"You haven't got any fucking money do you?"

He wasn't as dumb as orc-kind usually were.

"No. I don't."

"That's alright," he said. "I'll pay for it. But I think you and I had better have a chat before we meet up with the others."

GALAN DIDN'T LIKE horses. They were big, stupid, and prone to getting spooked every time he came up to one. Yet here he was, walking around one with a hand on his chin, pretending he had the slightest clue what he was doing.

"You want a look at her teeth?" The grizzled old ostler

made it sound like both a question and a suggestion.

Of course, the teeth. You wanted a horse to have good teeth because they bite. How far was he from the safety of the fence? *Squelch*. And why did they let the beasts just shit in the yard where prospective buyers would need to walk?

"And you say you don't have any full-white ones?" Galan worked his way around to the front of the beast, trying to appear comfortable being so close to such an unwieldy animal.

The horse looked at him with its dead, dark eyes and whinnied.

"I've been in this business thirty years," the ostler said. "I've never seen a pure white horse. Where'd you say you come from?"

Galan peered up at the horse's mouth. There were a lot of teeth. "South. Orthendine."

"And they have white horses down there?"

"Yeah, sure. It's a good horse." They'd need to paint its hind quarters, but it would otherwise play the part of a unicorn. Once they'd found a horn. "How much do you want for it?"

"She's seventy-eight gold coins. I'll throw in a saddle for another twenty."

"I'm not going to ride it. I'll give you seventy."

"She's not a drafting horse, not sure if she could pull a cart either. Seventy-five."

"No, I'm just going to walk her around a bit." Galan clapped his hands. "Deal. Can you keep it here for the afternoon? An associate of mine, an elven fellow, will come by later with the money."

"Fair enough."

Well, now they were getting somewhere. A lick of

whitewash and a... something strapped to the beast's head and they'd have a damn good fake unicorn. He just hoped it would be enough to fool the right people.

Galan walked away, gazed up at the stone buildings that crowded the narrow streets, and felt the tension in his shoulders dripping away. While these weren't the dirt and cobblestone roads of his adoptive city, they were still *streets*, and they still held *his* kind of people. Maybe restarting the guild in Threerun wasn't such a good idea, maybe it would be better to start here, right underneath the throne? At least the Sentinels here wouldn't know him...

He couldn't do that. Not unless he could convince Grog to move up here with him. Though their partnership was crumbling, there was still a solid bedrock of time beneath them. Surely that would count for something in the end, when it all came out. Moving to Kalindar might be just what was needed to reinvigorate both of them.

When he reached the market square, he found a seat near a fountain and waited. It seemed like a busy day today, good weather, lots of smiling faces. The stalls were arranged in little outward facing clumps, with the merchants at the centre. Most of the clumps had a private guard standing or walking around. The market was surrounded by permanent shops, whose owners would have purchased all the decent foodstuffs for resale, leaving what remained on display here wilted or brown.

He grinned at seeing a dirt-covered little girl bump into an elderly man bartering at a grocer's stall. No doubt she'd take the purse off to whoever housed and fed the orphans and other undesirable children of the city. Likely some old bandit who'd had enough of risking his own life for a few measly copper pieces. And she'd be thankful he cared for her and her friends.

Because no one else would. Even here, right below the Queen's own balcony, children were forced into a life of petty crime. At least when he ran things in Threerun they were given an education and an opportunity to do something else, though most grew up and became lifelong ne'er-do-wells. But he'd given them options.

What was the point of royalty if they couldn't make their subject's lives better?

"There he is." Elvalor broke Galan's reverie. He sat down next to Galan. "We're in."

Jendora stood in front of them, though there was room enough for her to sit too. Galan moved over a little bit by invitation, but she remained as she was. It felt like there was a lot of general hostility amongst the crew on this job, everyone was trying to prove they were tough and in charge. This was why there needed to be a guild, a hierarchy, so everyone knew their place.

"Just like that?" Galan knew he could rely on Elvalor talking his way into the party.

"We're a five piece band from Southport. Hired by a man named Soladar."

Galan raised an eyebrow. "And who is Soladar?"

"He is one of Count Radu's newest aides, tasked with finding the best entertainment for the annual party. No one can recall having met him, but he *is* only new."

That was two problems down. "Excellent."

"That's not all," Jendora said.

"Oh?"

Elvalor opened his purse and showed Galan the gleaming contents. "We've been paid in advance."

"Great. That's going to come in handy. I'm not sure how much I can push Lady Heatherdown to pay for everything. It wasn't part of the arrangement, she was only to pay on delivery."

"You sure she's got the money?" Elvalor didn't seem as agitated as before, but Galan recognised the attempt to have him say more than he should.

"Yeah, she's got the money. I've already seen it," he lied.

Jendora and Elvalor visibly tensed. Were they about to start a fight?

Galan slapped his knees as he stood. "Okay, let's go and find Grog and the druid. It's time we discussed the plans in more detail."

"There's one other thing," Elvalor said.

Jendora crossed her arms and got in Galan's way.

"What's that?" Galan asked, sitting back down. He slipped a throwing knife into each palm and kept them hidden from view.

"Janu," Elvalor said. "That Sentinel bitch followed us right under the mountain. That wasn't luck, she knew where she was going."

"Yes, I know," Galan said. "She's been following us since we left Threerun. Probably has a wizard scrying this very conversation."

"That's bullshit and you know it," Elvalor said. "The sentinels haven't any wizards on staff and they don't have the funding to pay for a long term scry."

Galan shifted on the seat. "You never know, she's got some dwarf working for her too now. Besides, maybe it's personal for the wizard, you know? Doing it pro-bono to get back at one of us for some perceived slight."

"You talk well," Elvalor said. "But not as well as me. You're grasping."

Their position next to the market, with Jendora blocking

the way, seemed suddenly very private. Anything could happen here, and if Elvalor was swift enough, no one would notice Galan's cut throat until he was already dead.

Galan edged the points of his blades past the edges of his fingers. "You trying to tell me you're an informant?"

"I'm no informant," Elvalor said. "And Jendora here only just joined us."

"It's gotta be Grog," Jendora said. "He's working for the Sentinels."

Grog you fucking idiot you're going to get killed!

Galan laughed and let the knives fall back into his sleeves. "Grog?! Don't be silly. It's me. I'm the informant."

THIEVES WERE THE same no matter what city they skulked about. They always sat with their back to a wall and their eyes in constant motion. Looking to see if they were being watched? Maybe. Janu thought they were more likely to be judging the best possible escape route, deciding ahead of time which rat-hole they'd sprint down when she came bursting onto the scene. At least, that's how she remembered the life.

And there the thieves were now, plaguing the Queen's own market, looking over their shoulders and trying to blend in. Galan's jabbing fingers and Elvalor's crossed arms made the argument obvious, but so far they'd managed to not devolve into violence. Maybe the dwarf woman's presence was keeping them civil.

"What do you make of it?" Janu asked Ainsworth. His level-headedness had him plan for her and Marrid's arrival well. As soon as she was spotted by the city guards, a message was relayed that brought them to this empty room above a bakery, where they had a good overwatch of the market square. Ainsworth had done well to keep tabs on

Galan from the moment the thieves arrived.

"Some kind of falling out?" he guessed.

"Maybe. It's hard to tell," Marrid said. "For all we know they might be talking about the weather."

"How so?" Ainsworth asked.

Marrid expelled air from his nose. "The thieves' guild often disguises their conversations in public like that. People give angry folk a lot of room, especially while they're arguing."

"Oh, so if anyone is listening they stick out by not moving on..." Ainsworth nodded in thought.

"What did you say that dwarf's name was?" Janu asked.

"Jendora." Though his voice was always level, Marrid said the name without any inflection at all, without any hint of emotion. "She's an exile."

Kalindar was full of dwarves that didn't meet the standards of the mountain homes. Most became drunkards and beggars, worse than thieves. Marrid's careful speech was clear, this Jendora was special.

"So." Janu added a hint of exasperation to her voice, urging Marrid to just get out with it. "What's her story, who is she to you?"

Marrid turned his head to her, but she kept hers pointed squarely at the market. Whatever it was, his initial hesitation was enough for Janu to know this wasn't easy for him.

"She is nothing to me. She is an exile, a deserter." After a moment he stared back down at the market. "She's a tracker, and a caver."

"What did she do to be exiled?" There was clearly a history here he didn't want to talk about, but Janu needed to know who she was dealing with.

"She broke a vow. One that shouldn't have ever been made in the first place. And she fled before facing judgement."

"Like a marriage vow?" Ainsworth interjected.

Marrid was silent for a moment. "Yes. She was my sister, once. But she blasphemed before Whurgan himself, desecrated one of his temples. The shame she brought upon our family, upon me, is the reason I was assigned this *diplomatic* duty."

Ordinarily, Janu would have sent him home. Any Sentinel with that much of a personal stake in a case couldn't be relied upon, let alone trusted. But Marrid was different. Dwarves were different. Stories of their honour systems were well known by anyone with a passing knowledge of dwarf-kind, to say nothing of their obsession with family and clan. She was sure this wouldn't stop him doing his job, but...

"Is this going to be a problem?" She had to be sure.

"No. But I do ask that if the opportunity presents itself, I will escort her to the mountain homes to face judgement."

Galan and Elvalor's gesticulations became more pronounced. A few peasants' heads swivelled with interest as they walked by. The thieves shot them deadly glances and leaned forward to speak. Jendora took a step toward the people meandering by and surveyed the market, appearing uninterested in what was being discussed.

"What's your assessment of the situation, Ainsworth?" Janu asked.

"Sir, I think they're struggling. Galan is the only professional criminal, along with Grog. With all our recent arrests, I think they've been forced to bring in outside help. Some of these guys are amateurs."

That was a good take. They were clearly arguing about something… what she wouldn't give to have a wizard scry them. "Do you know where they're staying?"

"Not really," Ainsworth said. "But there's not too many places in town. I would've had help from the Sentinels stationed here, but I did as you said, I haven't announced our presence."

"Good, let's keep it that way." No need to give someone else the chance to steal this victory from her. "Did you find your mother?"

"Yes, of course. She's ready to help whenever we need."

"Glad to hear it. Find out where these bastards are staying. I think we'll pay them a visit tonight."

HEATHER WATCHED AS the old woman raised her shaking hands to implore the skies above. Of course, with Grog towering over her hunched frame, there wasn't much sky to implore. Still, she continued.

"Oh, look around you," the old woman said. "Please. Times are tough, not many people come down this way since the Queen's Road was fixed up."

She was right, the dirt and puddle-filled street was vacant aside from a grumbling dwarf sitting in a gutter. Why didn't the people clean up this street, or remove it to allow the buildings to grow? Every other creature constantly recycled and refreshed the tunnels and paths in their nests.

"You're not helping your case," Grog said. "Why would I pay more for a shopfront with no foot traffic?"

The old woman straightened far more than Heather thought her back should be capable of.

"I'm not daft. And I know how to keep my mouth shut." She held her hand out and fixed her eyes on the orc.

Grog dropped a handful of coins into the shaking hand of the old woman. They'd haggled for longer than necessary, but she appeared to enjoy the game of it. Judging by the way she clinked the coins together as she walked away, she was happy with the outcome.

"Alright," Grog said. "Let's go on upstairs and talk about what we do next."

We. What did he mean by that? Her lack of funds to pay for the job wasn't a *we* problem, it was a *her* problem. By all accounts he should be livid… or maybe the druidic council was wrong once again? Maybe civilised people cared about more than just money?

Or maybe this was like the deceit of an angler fish, drawing her in before striking. Either way, she needed these people to get her into Count Radu's home. She reached her mind out and touched Legs's thoughts. *Come, be ready,* she told it. That was about as complex a command it would understand, if it even cared to listen to her.

The shop they just rented was the single largest building Heather had ever been inside. It was like a cave at first, dark, and cool, but with so much timber it also reminded her of a thicket in winter — only not as wet. She knew, of course, that it was supposed to offer safety from the elements, safety from the wild, but to her it felt like so much more than that. It felt like a home, something she could have complete control over.

"So." Grog lit a candle on a small table. "What exactly are you about? Did you think the Thieves' Guild would free a unicorn out of the goodness of their hearts?"

She looked for somewhere to sit, but there were no other chairs aside from the one Grog was lowering himself into.

"No," she said. "I just haven't been entrusted with the money." Lies weren't against the druidic teachings.

His jaw shifted to the side as he leaned back. Before he could speak she continued.

"And what about you? Why haven't you brought my lack of funds to the attention of the others?"

"Well… things aren't exactly as they seem. You see, I've been working for the Sentinels, leaving a trail for them to follow us."

That explained how the Sentinels were able to track them despite her efforts. But what did that mean for her and her plans?

"Why?"

"Before I joined up with Galan and started the guild, I used to be a city guard. I was good at it too, you know? Big ugly guy like me, not many people are willing to mess with an orcish fellow.

"But Galan had grand ideas. And I believed him. So then the Thieves' Guild rose up from the shit-filled gutters and we practically ran everything." He paused and used a finger to rub the inside of his ear.

Heather felt Legs on the outside of the building, questing for a way into it. "So what happened?"

"It got too big and Galan didn't know when to stop. By that time I had a family, secreted away in Lavender; I didn't want Galan or anyone else to know about them. Got a litter of pups there. So when the Sentinels came crashing down around us, I felt the wind change, like I did when I teamed up with Galan, and I turned." He switched his finger to the other ear.

Legs was inside now, in the ceiling rafters of the second floor.

"What do you want with me?"

"I want out. I want out of the guild. Out of the city. Out of the reach of the Sentinels. I want to be a druid."

"You what?"

He wiped his finger on the underside of the table. "I've done some research. Goblins, orcs, kobolds... *all* the wild-races have long histories of nature worship. I've always liked being outdoors, I take my kids into the forests around Lavender all the time, even if they are only one-quarter orc-blood, they still love it. It comes naturally to me, and if I'm a druid, I can be out of the shit for good.

"All I need is an introduction. I can't just sign-up like I did with the city guard."

If Heather's plans came to fruition, recruiting a prospective druid would ease the inevitable tensions with the council. They'd probably still come after her, but maybe it could help her to just be left alone. If they caught her.

"Alright. I'll introduce you to the council."

Grog let out a long sigh that rattled in his chest. At first Heather thought it was just the weight of all his troubles finally being lifted, but after a few moments his head slumped forward. A hooked, black leg rose up over his shoulder.

"Legs! No!"

CHAPTER SIX

Jobs

"WHAT HAPPENED?" GALAN hefted Grog's arm with two hands and let it thump to the floor. Although Grog didn't *look* dead — Galan had seen enough dead bodies in his time to know what one looked like — he also didn't seem alive.

Jendora glanced down and kicked Grog's foot. "Is he dead?"

"No," Heatherdown said from the other side of the room. "No he's not dead. He's just paralysed." She was peering behind the store counter.

Had Lady Heatherdown discovered that Grog was working for the Sentinels? Is that why she'd put him in this trance? How much did she know?

"What have you done to him?" Galan tried to sound accusatory and hurt, maybe the others would get on his side and help him protect Grog. They'd believe him over her, he'd already confessed to being an informant. But what then? She was the job... and these guys wanted to get paid. "You unsightly, scruffy-looking wench, I—"

"—It wasn't me! It was Legs. He thought I was in danger, and he was hungry, and Grog is a very big fellow..."

"Why did that godforsaken spider think you were in danger?" Jendora asked.

Elvalor stepped forward and spoke for the first time since entering the shop. "Is he going to be alright?" He searched the ceiling. "Where is Legs?"

"I don't know," Heatherdown said. "When I went to look for you guys he must have run-off. I screamed at him pretty loudly."

"Fuck. Okay." Galan sat on the floor and nursed his forehead in his palms. So she didn't know Grog was the informant. Good, one less problem to worry about. Only now he needed to get Grog out safely, while pretending to be the informant for Jendora and Elvalor's benefit, and preferably make it out with the unicorn as well.

"Are we still on?" Elvalor asked Galan. "We don't need Grog. He wouldn't make a convincing drummer anyway."

Shit. "No, we need him in case things get hairy. Besides, he's a much better lock-pick than me."

Elvalor scoffed. "Yeah, but we don't plan on running into any guards."

"I can handle guards if it comes to that," Jendora said. "The job isn't worth abandoning over one orc."

"Who said we're abandoning it?" Heatherdown joined the others in the centre of the room. She furrowed her brow at Galan. "Surely you can get me in the castle without Grog?"

"We don't really have a plan." Galan lifted his head. "Not a full one. We've got a way in, we got a decoy, but we don't know anything about the interior, or even where Radu's holding the unicorn. For all we know, we need Grog."

Everyone nodded appreciatively.

But this wasn't going to work. Sooner or later, the others would uncover the truth and turn on Grog. Galan had to get them both out of this.

"Plus you've got the Sentinels running around," Jendora said. "So you can feed them some bullshit and divert them elsewhere while we make our escape."

"So let's get to scouting," Elvalor said. "Why are we sitting around here?"

"Hold on." Heatherdown raised a hand. "What do you mean, 'you've got the Sentinels running around'?"

Elvalor smiled and gestured to Galan on the floor. "Galan here, master criminal that he is, has been feeding the Sentinels information. They think he's an informant. That's how they followed us down into the cave."

"I see." Heatherdown took a step back and turned away from the group.

"How long until Grog wakes up?" Galan asked her.

"I don't know," Heatherdown replied over her shoulder. "Normally Legs eats whatever he bites. I've never tested his venom."

"Where is Legs?" Elvalor asked again while searching the corner of the room behind him.

"Last I felt, he was heading toward the castle," Heatherdown said.

"What's he want at the castle?" Jendora asked. "He isn't going to cause any problems there is he?"

Heatherdown turned back to face them and shrugged. "He's just a stupid spider. It's probably because the castle is big and tall."

That was the opening Galan needed. "We can't have him risk the job. You three head to the castle, find Legs and stop him from doing anything. If the guards see him, they might increase their usual patrols. And if they warn Radu, the party might become very hard to sneak out of."

Jendora rolled her eyes. "That hardly takes all three of—"

"—while you're there," Galan added. "Scout the place. Walk around the exterior walls, note the distances, any towers, windows, balconies that you see. Get a rough map. If you can draw in any visible guard patrols it will help."

"What about you?" Elvalor asked.

"I'm going to stay here, plan things out... and look after Grog." *And get him and me the fuck out of this mess of a job.*

AINSWORTH DODGED A cart as he barrelled down the street toward Janu and Marrid. "Sentinel Janu! Some of the thieves are headed toward the castle."

"Are you daft?!" Janu hissed at him. "We're keeping a low profile, there's no telling how many spies they've got."

The good head on his shoulders checked the surrounding people moving about in the shade of the buildings. She stepped to the side, drawing him in to stand next to Marrid. Hopefully they now appeared as nothing more than friends talking on a busy street.

He lowered his voice. "I'm sorry," he urged. "But they're making a move on Radu now. If we hurry we can—"

"—don't be stupid, boy," Marrid cut in. "They're not making a move. They need to case the place out first."

If Marrid was willing to take his armour off or lower his war axe for just a moment, they would look a lot more like friends talking in a busy street. No matter what Janu said, he refused, and she couldn't order him. She placed a hand on his axe-head and pushed down on it.

"Would you please lower your axe? Every damn cutpurse or shoplifter in the city is going to run screaming to those thieves if they get a look at you."

The axe moved down, but he still held it in two hands.

"What should we do, Janu?" Ainsworth asked. He was starting to catch his breath.

"Is Galan with them?"

"Um, no. No. It was the dwarf woman—"

"—Jendora," said Marrid. "Her name is Jendora."

"Right." Ainsworth shook his head. "Jendora, Elvalor, and Lady Heatherdown."

Unusual that neither Galan or Grog were checking Radu's mansion out, considering they were the only two professional thieves in the group. "How long were they all in there?"

"Not more than twenty minutes," Ainsworth said.

Janu paused for a moment. "Then Grog and Galan are still in there? Alone?"

"Unless they came down past here, they're still in there."

"Alright," she said. "You two follow the others, keep an eye on them. Take note of anything they pay particular attention to. We need to know how they plan on getting in there, and how they plan on getting out. A unicorn isn't small, you can't just walk out with it."

"And what about you?" Marrid asked.

"I'm going to have a chat with Galan and Grog."

Marrid almost lowered the axe completely. "Are you sure that's a good idea?"

"Yes."

She'd almost forgotten, once again, that Marrid wasn't an official Sentinel. Ainsworth would never question her decisions as openly as that. Her plan was to goad Galan and Grog into action, force them to act before they were ready, help them make a mistake. And while she was talking with them, she might be able to glean a little more info. But that wasn't something neither Marrid nor Ainsworth needed to know.

Ainsworth and Marrid still stood there.

"Get a move on!"

After the two had trotted away, Janu set off down the street. Kalindar city, like most of the cities in the kingdoms, was a predominantly human city. And if the person shuffling about in a nearby shadow wasn't human they were probably a half-breed elf or orc. Halflings and dwarves were rare, but rarer still were her own kind, gnomes.

She'd become a fixture on the streets of Threerun for so long she'd forgotten what it was like to be stared at. Here in the streets surrounding the castle, they hadn't seen a gnome marching along, catching rapists and murderers, thieves and burglars; and so they eyed her with open curiosity.

There was no way she, Marrid, and Ainsworth had remained inconspicuous, and so no point in continuing the charade. The thieves knew they were followed as far as Kalindar anyway. Besides, subterfuge was never really Janu's style.

Sight of the storefront gave her pause. He was in there. The master criminal whose capture and imprisonment had eluded her for so long. Soon she would grab his arm, twist it behind his back, and declare him arrested in the name of the Queen. She just needed to know what he was planning. Any clue, any hint, could break open the case.

For a moment, she wondered if it was best to kick the door in, or walk in casually. She decided on the former. The door crashed open, rebounding off the inner wall. She kicked it again, breaking one of the hinges. Splinters flew through the dusty air.

"Excuse me, I'm looking for a den of thieves!" She laughed at her own wit.

Galan sat on a chair at the edge of the room, beside a simple wooden table. The sizable body atop it could only be Grog. Her entrance had caught the thief off-guard, but he didn't rise from his seat, and made no attempt to run.

But he was a lot smarter than a common criminal. He knew she had nothing on him, so he had no reason to run. Still, she thought he'd at least produce one of those blades he was so fond of.

"Janu." He sighed. "It's only you. What do you want?"

Grog hadn't moved a muscle. Though her eyes were still adjusting to the dim interior, the prone body didn't look right. The skin seemed too tight against the muscle underneath.

"I'm here on official Sentinel business. Heard you were planning a big job in the capital. I don't suppose you want to tell me about it... what's wrong with Grog?"

"He's a little under the weather. Spider bite."

"Well, I'm sure he'll be well enough in time for whatever you're planning."

"You mean you don't know what we're planning?"

She needed to play things carefully here. Did he *know* she didn't know, or was he fishing to see if she knew? Maybe he suspected an informant in his midst, and if she said something it would confirm it for him. The last thing she wanted was for them to abandon the job; this was her last best chance of arresting him. She needed to throw him off.

"I know all sorts of things," she said. "I'm here aren't I? But I'm only here to say 'goodbye'. I've been ordered back to Threerun."

His head perked up. "Is that right?"

"Yes. But I've informed the Sentinel Captain here to keep an eye on you."

"Would you like some company on the way back?"

Janu raised an eyebrow as she moved around and got a better look at Grog. That was one sick thief. "Pardon?"

"Grog and I will be heading back," Galan continued. "I think we're done being thieves."

What?!

"I know Grog has been feeding information to you." Galan watched her.

Grog?! The second in command was Ainsworth's informant?

"The others suspect him," Galan said. "It's time for us to pull out, find a new city. We won't bother you again."

"You can't!"

Galan studied her. Grog stirred.

"I mean... Y—You... Think of the money!"

"Janu, what are you talking about?" he said. "I thought you would be pleased we're hanging up the gloves."

Grog's hand lifted a half-inch from the table. Galan didn't seem to notice.

What could she do? They needed to continue the job until she could arrest them. If they gave up and walked away... where did that leave her? If she had to accept the rest of her career sitting behind a desk reading reports, she at least wanted this one big bust to look back on.

"I thought you could use a hand stealing that unicorn," she said.

Galan stood from his chair. "...what?"

"I don't get paid enough to try and stop you thieves, only to have you all get away richer than ever—"

"—We're completely broke."

"Not all the time though. And this time, I can guarantee you get away. I just need to get paid, I deserve that much."

The leader of the Thieves' Guild kept his eyes on her as he chewed his lip. Grog groaned and attempted to roll, drawing Galan's attention to the table.

"Alright." Galan checked Grog's pulse. "You keep the Sentinels off our back, and we'll cut you into the take."

"No."

"No?"

"Let's get something clear," Janu said. "You're working for me now. Understand? You cut me into the take, or I'll make sure every Sentinel across The Three Kingdoms has a sketch of the two of you."

Annoyance passed across Galan's face. "Fine. Don't you want to know how much your take is?"

"...How much?"

"I'll slip you a hundred gold coins."

Did he think so little of her to low-ball that far? Ainsworth had said a unicorn was worth several hundred platinum coins. "A hundred platinum," she said.

Galan's eyes widened with surprise, then he looked down at Grog. He furrowed his brow. "Deal," he said at last.

That was easy. Did he just rip her off? Janu shook her head clear. It didn't matter. What mattered is they were going to keep on with the job, she might learn a little something more of their plans, and she'd make the big arrest. There were five of them to bring charges against... she'd need some more Sentinels.

"So?" Galan asked. He'd been saying something but Janu hadn't been listening.

"So what?"

"Grog's name isn't on the books anywhere? Only you

know his identity?"

"Wha— oh yes! Only I do. The Sentinels have strict confidentiality rules regarding informants. I couldn't tell anyone else who the informant was even if I wanted to."

"Good. You keep it that way, and we'll cut you in on any future criminal enterprises we undertake."

"Of course."

"And we'll feed you some lower-level criminal activity every month or so, and once a year we'll give you something major. Something to keep your career going smoothly, so long as ours stays smooth."

Even though this was all a ruse, Janu still felt dirty discussing corruption so openly like this. Is this how it was spoken about? She'd half-imagined the wording would be more implied and covert. Criminals really weren't very clever, or at least the ones she grew up with were cleverer than this.

"Excellent!" Galan clapped his hands.

Grog's eyes fluttered open as he moaned, still trying to raise his hand from his side.

"You best be off," Galan said. "We'll keep our arrangement between you and me. No one else needs to know."

"No. For both our sakes, it stays between the two of us." Janu gave a quick nod and rushed out the broken door.

As she paced up the street toward the room Ainsworth had secured for them, she couldn't help but smile. It worked. That idiot! He really believed she'd turn like that for a few coins under the table. Oh the look on his face when she's there, waiting for him to lead that unicorn away, with a squad of men ready to make the arrest.

She could hardly wait.

* * *

LICHEN WAS THE sort of plant... thing... you never really forgot, even if you wanted to. Unlike a tree, or grass, lichen didn't have a coherent thought. Instead, it was a torrent of ideas and feelings — none of which seemed to share any relevance to any other — that overwhelmed the mind and threatened to drown you out.

So when Heather ran her fingertips along the stone wall surrounding the castle district and found intelligible fear instead of the usual stream of lichen consciousness, she paid attention.

What are you afraid of? She asked it.

Our homes! Someone is destroying us! You have to help!

Homes? What the hell was it talking about? Lichen didn't have a home, it just sort of... infected rocks like on this beautiful stone wall.

What are you on about?

Before the lichen could formulate a response, Heather felt a short vibration in the ground. Jendora and Elvalor were craning their necks up at the wall, scanning for Legs as well as scouting the area.

"Did you guys feel that?" she asked them.

Elvalor furrowed his brow. "What? Feel what?"

"Masons," Jendora said in a flat tone. "They're mending the wall. Knocking off old stones and replacing them."

Another vibration moved up through Heather's feet. "Let's go take a look," she said. "They're making the lichen unhappy."

Why were they both looking at her like that? Oh, right... these people didn't know about lichen.

Heather continued. "And if there's a broken bit of wall, it might be a good way in. Don't you think?"

Elvalor and Jendora shrugged, then proceeded down the narrow, inclined road that followed the inner wall. The two of them walked close together, speaking so Heather couldn't overhear, casting glances made to look innocuous back at her. A single word, 'money', made it to her ears. Had they figured out her lack of coins too?

As she contemplated asking a passing starling to relay the hidden conversation to her, a timber... *thing* appeared as they rounded the corner. At first, Heather wasn't sure what it was, but seeing the team of men, the ropes, and the amazing pulley system made it clear. They'd built, out of ash and birch, a network of platforms that allowed them to easily scale and work on the wall.

Nothing in nature did that. It was more confirmation that she belonged somewhere like this, where you could leave behind something that would last for eternity. Somewhere *progress* was made instead of the endless cycle of life.

"It's called 'scaffolding'," Elvalor said. "It's a temporary thing so they can work on the exterior of tall buildings."

"I know what it is," Heather lied. "I'm not an idiot."

Jendora pointed up the scaffolding. "There he is!"

Legs walked the underside of a length of ash about halfway up the wall. Beneath him, a short man — not a halfling but he'd feel comfortable around them — was scraping grey clay off a flat tool into a gap between the wall's stones. Spindly legs reached down and brushed the man's hair, seeking the underside of his jaw.

No. You stop that right now.

With a start, the spider curled itself back onto the beam, the man none the wiser.

Go back to the building where we were before. Stay there.

The spider crossed to the topside of the beam, out of view.

Where are you going? It's that way. Heather pointed out into the city as she glared up at the men working. *I'll get you a cat to eat, you like cats.*

"Where did it go?" Jendora asked. "And what are you pointing at?"

"He's not listening." Heather let her arm fall. "He's too stupid to learn anything. If we don't catch him, I'm not sure what he's going to do."

"I'll tell you what he's going to do," Elvalor said. "He's going to get spotted, and then they're going to lock the place down and send in a bunch of hunters to kill him."

"Don't worry," Heather said. "They won't catch him."

Elvalor waved his hand at her in a gesture she didn't fully understand. "I'm not worried about the fucking spider. I'm worried about them locking the place down and causing problems for us getting into the party."

"Oh."

"You're going to have to go up there." Jendora was still watching the wall. "He hasn't come out yet. Unless he can go invisible, he's still up there on the fourth level."

Heather had never caught something against its will. As a druid, it just wasn't something you did. Either an animal wanted to do what you asked or not. Of course, animal *companions*, like Legs, were supposed to be more helpful... and the few druids who ate meat did so without informed consent, so trapping Legs wasn't without precedent. But she had no idea how to catch anything, let alone a big ugly spider.

"We're all going to have to go up there," she said. "I can't catch him on my own."

"Uh-uh." Elvalor took two steps back and held his hands out. "No."

"I'll help." Jendora squared her shoulders. "You go up that side, I'll go up this side." She glanced back at Elvalor. "You stay down here."

"Okay," Heather said. "Just make sure to grab him from behind. Otherwise he might bite."

Jendora stepped up to the bottom of the construction and found a hold. "What do I do if it comes straight toward me?" She tested her weight on the beam.

"Punch him?" Heather shrugged. "Just don't get bitten."

As they climbed, Heather kept a watch for any movement near Jendora. Legs surely wouldn't attack Heather, but he was a predator, and he might feel trapped. She tried to divine for Legs location, but the lichen still screamed bloody-murder in an endless stream of incoherence, drowning out everything else.

Heather passed a man working a metal implement into the stone, prying a rock loose. Another man was stirring the same grey clay substance she saw before in a bucket. A sack of powder lay open next to him. They made clay themselves? They didn't just dig it up out of a riverbank? What an ingenious world the cities were.

There he was! Skulking behind a pile of half-broken stones. She motioned for Jendora and pointed toward him.

"Oi. What the fuck are you doing!" A man called out below them.

One of the men working the wall turned and spotted Jendora. She ignored him and continued manoeuvring into position.

"Just a friendly bet is all," Elvalor explained down below. "They were both boasting about who was the better climber.

Well now they're at it."

"They can climb a bloody tree. Get off that scaffolding! You'll bring the whole fucking thing down!"

All the men working the wall were paying attention now. Some watched on with interest. More than a few started telling them, with fear-strained voices, to get down.

Heather swung herself onto the platform and pushed herself between two workers. Legs was right there, trying to creep away. She dashed and grabbed his hind, but a suddenly flailing giant spider was hard to keep steady, and she swung around, pointing the many limbs at the men.

They yelled and climbed onto the outside of the construction, dropping themselves down with fearful glances back up. The platform under Heather swayed and shook. More workers started shouting.

Something cracked and clattered on the road below.

"Get off! Everyone! It's going to collapse!" a voice below shouted.

Everything began to shake and wobble as the remaining people rushed down the scaffolding. A sudden jolt sent tools and buckets flying.

Heather couldn't sense any trace of Legs behind the cheering chorus of lichen. He must have run off somewhere.

After two successive bumps, something gave way and started to break down. As Heather tilted toward the ground, she sprinted and jumped off to the side. A nearby maple reached out and caught her, groaning with the effort. The sticks and branches hurt, but she was thankful all the same.

The tree plopped her to the ground just as the scaffolding crashed down. Plumes of dust rose into the air as fragments of wood and stone bounced along the ground. The smoke settled, revealing Jendora suspended halfway up the wall on a rope, lowering herself down. Elvalor stood a little ways back, mouth agape and wide-eyed. Heather walked up to him.

"Legs is gone," she told him.

His expression didn't change as he turned his eyes to her. "We need to go. Now!"

Jendora made it to the ground and jogged over. A group of six men, dressed in metal armour and brandishing swords came around the corner. The leader pointed at Jendora and sprinted toward her, the other men following close behind.

"Halt! In the name of the Queen!" the leader shouted.

The surrounding workmen held their arms out and blocked Jendora's escape. Just as Heather was beginning to think running away might be a good idea, a group of hard-faces surrounded her and Elvalor. Three men forced Elvalor's arms behind his back while two more stood in front of Heather ready to pounce if she made a move.

"You're all under arrest," the leader said as he broke through the crowd.

Heather lurched to the left then dashed into a gap between the soldiers. Armoured arms grabbed and dragged her to the dirt. She struggled, kicked, tried biting one, but couldn't get away.

CHAPTER SEVEN

Escape

THE SMALL ROOM above the bakery was hot, either from the sun outside or the ovens underneath. Sweat trickled down Janu's back, fraying her patience.

She ran her hand down the side of her face. "What do you mean they're under arrest?"

"It's crazy." Ainsworth rubbed the back of his head. "To be honest, I'm not sure what happened."

"What do you mean you're not—"

"—There's no sense in what they did," Marrid confirmed. "As Peter says, it was crazy. We were following a good distance behind as they paced the outer—"

"—Peter?" Janu threw her hands up at Marrid. She turned away and walked to the open window overlooking the market. It was a busy day, no doubt half the people down there were pick-pockets. Hot air blew past, carrying the unholy scent of a tannery. The last strand of her patience snapped. "Who the *fuck* is Peter?"

"That would be me." Ainsworth held a hand up.

"As I was saying," Marrid said. "We were following them. There was a crew of masons working on the wall. The three of them stood around for a bit, then brought all the scaffolding down."

These two needed to learn a little about clarity. "What scaffolding?"

"The scaffolding the masons were using," Ainsworth said. "For whatever reason, the thieves pulled it down."

"And were promptly arrested by the city guard," Marrid finished. "I need to take Jendora back home to face our courts."

There was only one way this could be any worse. "Are the local Sentinels involved?"

"No sir," Ainsworth said. "At least we don't think so. It was just the city guard."

"Thank fuck for that." Janu chewed her bottom lip. Galan and Grog couldn't pull off the heist without the others, even with her help distracting the Sentinels. Hells, without the druid there was a real risk Galan would give up. A unicorn couldn't be sold to just anyone, it was only worth something if you had a buyer lined up.

There was only one thing for it. "Okay. I'm going to go speak to the city guards and get the thieves released."

"You're what?" Marrid's face was the pinnacle of confusion, but then it eased into realisation. "I can still take her home," he said to himself.

"These charges don't mean anything." Ainsworth's good head was coming to the fore again. "Damage to public property, causing a disturbance. Aside from a fine and paying for the damages, they'll be out in a week anyway, why not a little earlier?"

"That's right," Janu nodded. "And they only have this

one opportunity to steal the unicorn. I'll get them released and then when they tell me their plan, we'll know exactly where to wait for them."

Marrid scoffed. "You think they'll tell you their plan in return for letting them go? They'd just lie and use it to manipulate us."

Ainsworth nodded.

"No." Janu folded her arms. "They think I'm working with them."

There was silence.

Janu continued. "They think I'm corrupt."

"You've got to be kidding," Marrid scoffed louder than last time. "This is what Galan does. He manipulates and works people like pieces in a game."

"No," Janu said. "Not me. I know what he's doing. He's got his own problems within their little thieving party."

"You're sure about this?" Concern pulled Ainsworth's lips down into a deep frown.

"Yes, but if it makes you feel any better, let's give Radu the heads up. Give him that teleportation orb so he can zap us in if he sees anything."

Marrid pulled at a bead in his beard. "You want to trust Radu with one of the orbs?"

"These are the only ones we have left," Ainsworth added.

"Yes." She'd had enough of them questioning her. "Where's your sorcerer mother?"

The sudden change in topic had Ainsworth stumble on his words. "I—err, I asked her to meet us here later this afternoon."

"Great. You all wait here. I'm going down to the guards."

Without waiting for any more arguments, complaints, or objections, Janu strode out the door and bounded down the stairs. She took the market-side exit and made her way to the city guardhouse, a large stone building, on the other side of the square.

It was, like most military buildings, ugly. The ceiling was too low for most residents and guards — her gnomish stature gave an advantage there — with nothing but the occasional slit in the stone to act as a window.

Heat radiated from the street. A shoeless child ran past, laughing, no doubt at whoever he'd just stolen from. Was she ever that carefree growing up in the gutters of Threerun?

The guardhouse's wooden door that faced the market was closed. Unsurprisingly, it wasn't locked — who would rob a guardhouse? — so she stepped in and announced herself.

"I am Sentinel Janu of Threerun. You have three prisoners arrested earlier today. They are to be released."

Too late, she realised she should have read the room before speaking. In front of her, three city-guards were standing in a circle with three Sentinels. The tallest one, a heavy woman — ugly enough to be part orc if not part troll — turned and crossed her arms. She hunched over under the oppressive ceiling.

"A Threerun Sentinel?" She raised an eyebrow at her two companions. "Why wasn't I informed?"

The two looked at each other and began to utter a response, but Janu cut in. "I didn't announce my presence. I am undercover."

The ugly Sentinel glanced at the three guards. "Well, you've blown your cover," she said to Janu.

"I had no option. Those prisoners are to be released."

"Now hold on." The ugly Sentinel unfolded her arms. "Why would we release them?"

"They are integral to my investigation. I need them to be free to—"

"—hold on," the ugly Sentinel cut in with a palm held up. She pointed to the three guards. "You three are on mandatory overtime and this guardhouse is shut down."

With a nod, the other two Sentinels moved to the exits and stood to attention, now guarding the guardhouse with its three hapless guards.

"The three of you may as well get comfortable, it might be a while," the ugly Sentinel informed the guards. "You've heard too much, so until this is all dealt with, you're stuck here. Anyway." She turned back to face Janu, ignoring the sounds of exasperation from the guards. "You were saying?"

"I need those prisoners free to go about their business. They are all under investigation for *serious* criminal enterprise. I am undercover. I want to arrest them for real crimes, but time is of the essence, they must be freed today."

If she were the Sentinel in charge of this city, she wasn't sure this would be enough to convince her. But she didn't want the glory of this arrest to go to anyone but herself. She'd worked too long and hard for this.

"They are already under investigation for serious crimes," the ugly Sentinel said. "Attempted regicide."

Regicide?! They weren't here to kill the queen. But of course, the Sentinel in the queen's own city had only one true concern: the Queen.

"You can't possibly be serious," Janu said. "They aren't after the queen. That's ridiculous. All they did was wreck some scaffolding."

"No. They were attempting to sneak a highly poisonous spider through the walls. A *giant* spider I might add, highly trained for assassination."

What the fuck was she talking about?

"What?" Janu shook her head. "I—I—I have no idea what you're talking about. Giant spiders? No... they're not after the Queen. They are trying to steal a unic—" Shit! She'd said too much.

"Unicorn? They're after Radu's unicorn? So they're thieves as well?"

"Not 'as well'. They're just thieves."

"I'll be sure to add conspiracy to commit theft to the charges. The Queen will be most pleased with another foiled assassination attempt. I just hope we can capture the spider in time."

Janu paced her words. "What fucking spider?"

"One of the city guards, Felor, sulking over there in the corner, spied it on the wall. A couple of the masons said they saw it too. Those three had something to do with it, trying to get it in through one of the holes the masons were working to fix."

"That doesn't make any sense. Spiders can climb. It would just climb the wall. They don't need to push it through a hole."

"Nevertheless." The ugly Sentinel strode over to a small table to pour herself a mug of water. "A spider was involved, and those people controlled it."

This was insane. Why were all Sentinels so difficult?

"You're not going to let them go are you?" Janu asked.

"Not a chance."

There weren't many options left... Could she go so far down this path... Janu closed her eyes and took a breath. The air was cooler here in the guardhouse. Sternness wasn't going to work on a fellow Sentinel; she needed to reign in her temper.

"Where are they being held?" she asked.

"In the Sentinel headquarters." The ugly Sentinel took a long drink. "Why?"

"That should be secure enough to keep them. I'm sorry that I won't get my arrest. But it's good that you've got yours."

The ugly Sentinel smiled, which seemed to only make her uglier. Janu turned and left without even asking for a name. Was she really going to break the thieves out of prison? There was no other way forward she could see.

Once she was outside the guardhouse, a cloud passed overhead and a fine rain started to fall. It did nothing but raise the humidity.

Unbelievable! Janu really *was* corrupt. All those years spent chasing shadows through the back-alleys of Threerun must have really done a number on her. But here she was, like any other corrupt official, reporting to him, Galan, Leader of The Thieves' Guild. When she came to him with the offer, he wasn't convinced. But now? Now he knew for sure that there was a price for *anyone*.

He took up the familiar bearing of his illustrious position, placing his feet up on the table. Sitting on the only chair in the room helped turn the barren little shop into something more akin to the storeroom of Franki's tavern, where he used to hold court.

Grog leaned against the wall and tried to hide his ill-health. That spider really messed him up. A lesser man may have died. Soon, he'd set things right with his friend.

"Thank you for bringing this to my attention," Galan said in his old leadership tone. "What do you plan to do?"

Janu swiped Galan's legs off the table. "Knock that shit

off. I'm not some city-guard letting your boys off the hook for rowdy behaviour."

With a slight, annoyed frown, Galan motioned for her to continue.

"Breaking them out of the Sentinel headquarters won't be easy," she said.

"It's never been done before," Grog said from the wall. His voice was soft enough so that nothing vibrated. "Not from the Sentinels."

"But you've never had a Sentinel on your side," Janu said. "I can get us in. But you two will have to get us all out."

You would think the Sentinels would be better at coming up with plans, but this wasn't much better than Galan's own attempts at strategies. When Janu came in here and suggested a breakout, the thought of having someone on staff who could devise clever schemes lifted a huge burden off Galan's shoulders. Having more people working on the big-picture ideas would've helped a lot in rebuilding.

No matter. The guild would rise again.

"I think we can handle that." Galan turned to look at Grog, expecting the same sure nod the half-orc always gave him at times like this. Instead, Grog held a hand against his head.

"We can definitely handle that," Galan confirmed. "We need to move fast though. Radu's party is tomorrow night."

Janu made for the door as though both he and Grog would follow. "We can go now," she said.

"Woah woah woah," Galan said. "You don't do a prison breakout during the middle of the afternoon."

"How would you know?" Janu whirled to face him, finger pointed. "To my recollection, you never broke anyone out of prison."

"Sure I did," Galan said.

"Not once did we ever have a missing—"

"—Violence doesn't always solve our problems." Grog moved off the wall and stepped up to Galan's side. "We usually send someone like Elvalor to 'break' our friends out."

"That's not going to work this time." Janu planted her feet apart. "The Sentinel who's got them is using them as proof of an assassination attempt."

Those idiots, what the hell were they thinking?

"And," Janu added. "You haven't got Elvalor to get them out. But you've got me."

Galan wanted to knock the smug little smile off her face. He stood up and stretched instead, broadcasting his nonchalance.

"Okay," he said. "We'll do it your way. When do we leave?"

"Now," Janu said. "The watch will change soon, and if we're in any luck, the Sentinels on duty might not have been given all the information. Easier to talk my way in."

Wow... the Sentinels really didn't think things through.

"And then what?" Galan asked. "How are we going to talk our way out with three prisoners?"

"I told you, that's your job," Janu said. "I can get you in. You get us out."

They *really* didn't think things through. He looked at Grog and shrugged. The half-orc looked a little better with the prospect of some violence.

"You know we're going to have to fight our way out," Grog said to Janu. "Sentinels are going to get hurt."

She glanced away and went still. This was the real test of loyalty. If she was willing to do this, she was in his pocket for life.

"Whatever we need to do," she said.

And she didn't even ask for more money. The new Thieves' Guild was going to be even bigger and better than the last one.

A JAIL CELL was very much like a cave. It was dark, and the air had that cloying scent of dampness that never went away. The guards acted how Heather was taught to expect of civilised people, gruff and bad-tempered. Her two companions were a little gruff too, and recent events had made them bad-tempered. But she'd gotten to know them somewhat… they weren't so bad.

Bird-song whistled through a tiny horizontal slit in the stone wall, just beneath the ceiling. It was at the outside's ground height, with a sheet of discolouration lining the wall under it, evidence of where the water went when it rained. Aside from the guard's candle-light coming from around the corner at the far end of the row of cells, the thin window was the only source of illumination. Heather wasn't sure, but reasoned that Elvalor's half-blood probably gave him some partial gift of the elven sight she enjoyed. Jendora could probably see better than Heather down here.

"Are you going to do *anything*?" Elvalor's voice came from the cell next to hers, closest to the guard. He'd been complaining since they got there… well, since the guard went around the corner to sit at his table and torture them.

This guard had a wood and sheep intestine device similar to Elvalor's. Since she'd first seen him checking over it, she had wondered what it was for, but didn't want to expose her ignorance by asking. Now she knew. It was designed to produce excruciating sounds at intermittent intervals.

Torture.

"Hello? Are you going to do anything?"

At least Elvalor wasn't complaining any more.

"Are you talking to me?" she asked, trying to sound cheerful. Without trees, grass, and sun, it was hard to not feel depressed down here. The guard made another screeching sound that shuddered up Heather's back. She winced.

"*Yes*!" Something clanked against metal bars. "I've seen some of your magic. Get us out of here."

As if she hadn't thought of that. It was the first thing she tried to do, but her connection to the natural world was weak. No doubt the metal bars and supports holding up this building were diminishing her abilities. Her mind flowed out through the ground beneath her feet, but the flagstone was thick and hard for her to penetrate. Only the faintest hint of root brushed the undersides. It wasn't enough.

"I'm sorry," she said. "I can't."

Jendora's voice came from the cell on the far side of Elvalor. "Can't? Or *won't*?"

What social faux pas had Heather unwittingly committed?

"There's too much between me and nature," Heather said by way of explanation. "If I can't touch the natural world, I can't use its magic."

Jendora scoffed. "Bullshit."

"It's not 'bullshit'."

"There are druids in the mountain homes who've spent their whole lives underground," Jendora said. "They have no problem working the stone to their will."

Dwarves must be stubborn to have the patience to get rock to do something. Heather had tried when she was first ordered to her little grove, but gave up after three months.

"Well I'm not a dwarf," Heather said. "I can't control rocks, let alone man-made ones."

"Well... turn into a rat and find a way out." Elvalor's cell bars rattled.

"What?"

"Or even better," Jendora added. "Go and get the key off the guard."

Wild Shape wasn't something a druid just *did*. It required a reason, a damn good reason, to take on the form of another living creature.

"I've never done it before," she said to her feet.

"No time like the present," Elvalor hinted.

"It's not that easy," she said. "If nature doesn't think I should transform, it won't allow me."

"No harm in trying," Elvalor said.

Jendora spoke loud enough to risk alerting the guard. "Just fucking *do it*."

A rat. Okay. Just a little rat. What harm could come from that? She felt down into the ground, but remembered there would be no connection to the natural world. It didn't matter, shape-shifting like this could be done without feeling the grass beneath her feet. But the second she was back on a normal surface, if the natural world didn't approve of what she'd done...

The cell exploded in height around her. Her arms and body were suddenly hairy and didn't feel right at all. A sensation confused her for a moment before she realised it was a tail. Only now did she remember the warnings of her instructors, about the stories of the druids who took to the form too well, and never turned back.

Not her. No way. This sucked.

Torturous sounds from the guard spiked at her ears. She

bolted out through the bars of the cell and squeaked involuntarily at the size of the once narrow hallway. It was like a city-street to her now. Better to get it over with quickly.

Off to her right she imagined Elvalor was looking down at her in shock and awe, but strangely, as a rat, she couldn't really make out much of his face. The instructors never told her the senses would be like those of the creature... Maybe they had never done it themselves? One more thing the council was afraid of.

An urge to eat whatever she could smell ahead of her almost took over her mind. She pushed the animalistic thoughts down and concentrated, rounding the corner. It was the guard and his lunch in front of her, sitting at a small table, lit by a few candles. The sheep intestine device was making it hard to think.

But where was the key? It was iron, and hung by a ring on his belt. Her little eyes squinted but she couldn't see it, or rather, her eyes wouldn't focus. The thought of snatching away some of that bread was too much.

The key. The key was food. Everyone knew that. You could eat those keys, they were tasty, like a nut.

There it was, right where she thought it would be. Why would anyone want to live out their days in a form like this? It was horrible. No wonder rats seemed so idiotic, and no wonder the druids were scared of this power.

Climbing up the chair wasn't a problem. It didn't feel like a vertical climb, it didn't even appear as though it was anything other than flat ground to her... just, flat in a different direction. The guard's leg was warm. She rubbed up against it as she moved toward the key, stopping every couple steps to fix her whiskers.

The horrid sounds had stopped. *Oh he's taking a bite!* It

looks really good. Some fell! *There, I can just reach up and take it.* Fuck! *What was that?* Ow! *Why did the wall fall on me?*

Danger! Something is coming!

The room shrunk around Heather, and she found herself laying on her back, watching the guard get off his chair and stop in his tracks. Her whiskers were gone, her tail was gone.

A blade touched her neck.

"What are you, a fucking wizard or something?" the guard asked. His face grimaced in anger. "Trying to kill a guard, give me a plague or something. That's a life-sentence for you I'd wager."

Plague? Why would she want to make him sick?

"Come on." His sword retreated just enough to let her prop herself up on her elbows. "Get up."

She moved slowly, rising on one arm and feeling the sword hover near her shoulder as she stood. The guard was shorter than her, but he made up for it by being considerably wider; parts of him spilled out of his Sentinel-rose chestplate.

"What now?" she asked. Surprised by her own confidence, she continued. "Do you think a sword is going to stop a powerful druid like myself?"

His foot took a step back, but planted itself firmly onto the stone floor. "I'll cut you before you can get a single spell off. Don't make a move."

Getting past him wouldn't be easy, there wasn't a lot of space to squeeze by, even if he wasn't holding a sword out at her. She reached into the ground beneath her feet, but still couldn't make a strong enough connection. With a shrug, she turned and walked back to her cell.

"Thought so," he said. "Probably the only spell you know, and now it's used up."

Despite the threat of the blade at her back, she kept her

pace slow as she turned the corner down to the row of cells. She glanced in at Jendora and then Elvalor. Both remained silent and neither seemed very pleased with what happened. At least she tried, they hadn't done anything except complain.

"Say, you know," Elvalor said as her cell door closed. "It strikes me that they don't treat you Sentinels with much respect."

"Come off it," the guard laughed. "One of us walks down any street in Kalindar and the crowd parts before us."

"Oh, of course. Odd then that you're left down here in the dark by yourself."

The guard huffed.

"Ample sunlight is needed for good health, you know," Elvalor said. "Why, a man stuck in the dark most his days is prone to all sorts of ailments. Illness and disease run rampant in the dark, as I'm sure you know."

"Yeah." The guard's footsteps stopped. "The number of you prisoners who've died from disease down here. I'm lucky I haven't gotten anything serious."

"Well, I'm sure if you're not getting the sunlight you must be getting fed a bloody good meal down here."

"How's that?"

"How else would you stave off infection? Must be a hearty three squares a day?"

The guard paused for a moment. "Nah. It's just bread with the odd bit of cheese. Maybe a strip of meat on a good day. Have to get all my decent meals at home." Hands slapped on his chestplate.

Elvalor scoffed. "Why that's not much better than what they feed us."

"Yeah," the guard said. "Not much better. Sometimes I

eat some of what I'm to feed you lot." He chuckled at his own joke.

Elvalor chuckled too. "I don't blame you. I'd do the same were I in your shoes."

Silence sat heavy.

"Must get boring down here too," Elvalor said. "Seems a bit quiet."

Boots scraped against stone. At the edge of what Heather could see out of the cell, the guard was now leaning against the wall opposite Elvalor's bars.

"It's a bit dull," the guard said. "I bring a book or a pamphlet or something to pass the time."

"A learned fellow?" Elvalor's voice went up a notch in disbelief. "I'd always taken the Sentinels to recruit only the most dull-witted."

The guard's nose scrunched up.

"That must be why they stationed you down here," Elvalor added. "Can't have someone too clever milling about and questioning the higher-ups, hey?"

"Yeah." The guard glanced down the hallway toward the exit.

"Say, you know what?" Elvalor's voice perked up. "A bit of music would pass the time down here. Was that you I heard plucking away?"

"Yeah that's right." The guard smiled. "Been passing the time down here with it."

"Can I have a go? I play a little myself."

"Well... I'm not supposed—"

"—of course, of course. I understand. You gotta stick to the rules, even if you're the one running the jail house."

The guard glanced at his feet and then looked up. "Fuck it. Hold on." He pushed himself off the wall and moved out of view, his footsteps trailing around the corner.

"What are you doing?" Jendora hissed.

"Just shut up," Elvalor said. "Don't say anything, and cover your ears."

As the guard walked back down the hall, he spoke to Elvalor. "Some poor sod left this down here after he caused a ruckus in a tavern one night. I haven't been able to get a decent tune out of the thing."

He held the rounded hollow box by its neck and passed it to Elvalor's outstretched hand. With a thunk and a murmured apology, Elvalor wove the device through the bars.

Elvalor struck the intestines. Heather cringed at the unpleasant sound resonating in the box.

"Oh, it's out of tune," Elvalor said. "That's probably why you're not getting much out of it."

Elvalor hummed and plucked each intestine string individually, a much more pleasing sound, which then wound its way to a higher or lower pitch. A few times two notes were played in unison, making a discordant sound that was soon turned into something Heather could imagine herself liking.

When the methodical process was finished, Elvalor made the box produce a harmonious sound by striking all of the strings. It felt like the sun breaking through the clouds and warming the grass. He did it a second time, covering the warmth of the sun with rain clouds.

"Right, that's better," Elvalor said.

The guard nodded encouragement. "Go on, play a tune."

The sounds that came from Elvalor's cell were strange. They started off like before, but singular notes intertwined with the full-sounding ones, creating a melody like birdsong.

Then something changed in the cadence, from the undulation of a smooth hillside into a crevice of twisted and gnarled trees. Heather tried to place each note in the correct order, convinced they were jumbled but soon found herself lost in it all.

Something in this wasn't right. She tried to ask a question but couldn't remember the right words, and managed to only utter nonsense. The guard watched her with wide eyes, and then jerked his head to the side as though he was trying to catch the same notes she was.

Through the fog of her thoughts, Elvalor said *something*. The music changed, and her body gave way. With her last thought, she reached her arms out in front of her to lay her head down. Darkness overtook her.

CHAPTER EIGHT

On the Run

JANU HELD HER chin high as she strode up to the two stories of stone and mortar that was the Kalindar Sentinel Headquarters. She was reminded of the first time she ever approached a Sentinel building, dragged against her will, kicking and screaming defiance. An orphan caught stealing the wrong purse. A lifetime ago.

The building nestled up against the wall that separated the wealthy district from the poor. No doubt the ugly Sentinel would rather it was on the other side, in its proper place amongst the nobility and well-to-do of the kingdom.

She'd expected to be challenged upon approach, but no guards were posted outside. This *was* the right building. Such lax security wouldn't fly in Threerun, Marrid would never have allowed it. She opened the doors and stepped into the dark.

The walls were bare stone, the mortar still rough and uneven without the exterior weather to smooth it. It must be new... What sort of political pull did the ugly Sentinel tug on to get funding for a new headquarters? No trappings of decor or personality were present. Just the oppression of flat grey bureaucracy.

An array of desks lined the walls, surely more than there were Sentinels, and still others were pooled in the centre facing each other. More than half were vacant, with dour-faced Sentinels sitting and shuffling papers at the others.

None of them looked up, noticed, or acknowledged her entry. This wasn't just lax security, this was poor administration. Marrid was a godsend.

Janu cleared her throat and poked her chin a little higher. A Sentinel glanced out the corner of his eye but quickly returned to her papers.

"I am Sentinel Janu of Threerun. You have prisoners I am to interrogate." In Janu's experience it was easier to get things done if you made it sound like you'd been ordered to do it.

Another Sentinel raised his head, saw her, then looked to his colleagues. When no one acted, he too turned back to what he was doing.

What was wrong with these people? "Who is in charge here?"

Before he could look away, Janu caught the eye of a half-breed elven Sentinel. "You. What is your name and rank?"

"Err...." His eyes darted around the room but no one came to his aid. "Officer Penhold. I umm, I'm busy. If you could just—"

"—Where are the prisoners kept?"

"You'll need to speak to the Captain. She'll be back from patrol soon."

Janu would get nowhere if forced to negotiate with the ugly Sentinel again. She took a step forward and crossed her arms. "I am Captain of the Threerun Sentinels. You will escort me to the prisoners at once."

"Sir—ma'am... I—I—"

Through even the flagstone floor, Grog's footsteps thrummed as he entered the building. Janu had told him and Galan to wait a few minutes before coming in behind, hopefully at the right time to reinforce the urgency of her demands.

"Oh good, you're here," she said to Grog.

After ducking through the doorway, he stretched himself up to his full height and put his hands on his hips. Galan popped out from behind him, twirling a slender knife around his knuckles.

"Where are the prisoners to interrogate," Galan asked her. "We'll get to the bottom of their assassination plans."

"Just a moment," she said to him. "There's some difficulty here."

Grog let his voice boom through the room. "What? We were ordered to come here immediately and interrogate. I do not want to return to the Captain empty handed."

Oh good, they must have been listening at the door. Shame that no one had told her the Captain's name, they couldn't refer to her as the 'ugly one'.

"There is an active plot against the Queen's life," Janu told the Sentinel in front of her. "There is no time to waste, we must get to the bottom of this."

The sentinel made furtive looks around the room. All the others were paying attention now, frozen with papers dangling from their hands and quills half-raised from the desk.

"We're not supposed to have anyone go down—"

"—Do you want to explain to the Captain why you

allowed an assassination attempt to go unanswered? Do you want to stop her from preventing another threat on the Queen's life?"

"No. No." He steeled himself and rose from the desk. "Follow me, please."

A door at the back of the room took them to a hallway lined with offices. Although she could only glance in each as they walked by, they appeared identical, right down to the corner of the room the desk was in and the size of the stack of papers awaiting someone. But none of them had anyone in them. Things were definitely done differently in Kalindar. Why were all the junior officers present but all the senior ones out?

The hallway ended in steps leading both up and down. Officer Penhold grabbed a lantern from the wall, lit it from a candle and led them under the headquarters. As soon as they were beneath the ground, Galan appeared beside Janu.

"Sentinel Janu, I will need easy access to an outdoor area to interrogate the prisoners."

That was quick thinking, but did he really think the Sentinels would be so stupid that they'd allow that? She shrugged, it was worth a shot.

"Penhold, is this the only way down to the cells? We need open air to break these would-be assassins' minds."

Penhold glanced back at them as his feet reached the bottom of the stairs. There was a short hallway running from left to right, walls and floors of tight-packed stone, with metal-braced doors at both ends. Familiar scents of earth and damp hung heavy in the air, making it difficult to breathe. Janu missed her own headquarters, where she'd organised new construction to cycle the stale air.

"There's a service door down that way," Penhold said,

holding the lantern off to the left. "Comes out into the training yard. Should be room enough there for what you need." He sounded like he was going to ask the last part as a question, but changed his mind halfway through. "The err... prisoners are this way."

In front of the door, Penhold thumped three times and waited. After a moment he thumped again and called out. "Come on Bernard. Put that thing down and open the door."

When no response came, Grog stepped forward, hunched over under the low ceiling, and eased Penhold away. "Something isn't right," he declared.

Penhold pushed Grog's arm out of the way and produced a key from a pocket. "Get out of the way," he said.

Grog looked surprised, but Janu knew the Sentinels very rarely recruited cowards or people easily intimidated. They didn't always recruit the brightest, but that wasn't what they were after. How *had* this captain of theirs managed to hold such an iron grip on the city's law enforcement?

The door swung inward with a creak, revealing a dim room, with a small table and chair against the wall. Behind it, a hallway passed around a corner.

"Bernard, where are you?" Penhold called.

This time, Penhold hung back as Grog proceeded first, with Galan close behind. Janu stood in the doorway and waited.

"There's no one here," Grog announced.

Galan came back around the corner, twirling a blade away, and with a deep frown creasing his face. "The guard is asleep, missing his keys."

Penhold gasped. "An escape!"

He rushed toward the door.

Janu drew her sword and spoke in a whisper. "Not so

fast. We don't want to raise an alarm. If these people know they're being tracked they'll disappear forever."

"What? They'd already assume they're being tracked," Penhold said, his brow pulled down hard in confused anger. "If they make another attempt on the Queen—"

"What is the meaning of this!?" The ugly Sentinel boomed from the stairwell.

Holding a palm out to Penhold to keep him in place, Janu spun to see the ugly Sentinel heading toward her.

"Captain." Shit, why didn't she find out her name? "Officer Penhold here seems to have lost your prisoners."

"Janu, what are you doing here?" The ugly Sentinel demanded. "Penhold, I told you no one was to come down here."

"Sorry, sir—ma'am, I—"

"—And where the hell are the prisoners?"

"I don't know—"

"You." The ugly Sentinel redirected her attention back to Janu. "Who are these other people? What are you doing here?"

Galan stepped forward, gave a little bow and smiled. "Captain, we are interrogators, brought in by Sentinel Janu to try and ascertain whether there will be further attempts on the Queen's life."

"Shut up," the ugly Sentinel said. "Where are the prisoners?"

"Enough of this," Grog said. "They've escaped. We need to get a move on." He walked up the doorway and made to squeeze past the ugly Sentinel.

Steel flashed and a blade appeared, pointed at Grog's stomach.

"No one is going anywhere," the ugly Sentinel said. "Not

until I know what's going on."

"There's no time," Grog said, back-handing the blade to the side. "We need to go now."

"Too right." Galan leapt forward, ready to leave right behind Grog.

The ugly Sentinel kept the point of her sword raised as she took a step backwards. There was more room in the hallway for her to swing, and with the door between them and her, it was a well-defensible position.

From further in the room, the scrape of a sword being drawn rang out.

"Don't try anything," Penhold said.

Janu looked to Grog and Galan. They looked at each other and shrugged.

With an odd sense of ease, Grog stepped forward and punched Penhold in the chest. Something broke under the armour as the man slammed into the wall. He collapsed in a heap.

The ugly Sentinel was already upon them before Penhold's head hit the ground. Janu was sure the ugly Sentinel would stay where she was, in a defensive position, at least that's how the Sentinels in Threerun were trained. But she came through the door, shrieking and swinging her sword in a low, wide arc.

Sparks flew up from the sword-tip as it glanced along the ground and came up toward Grog's head. Galan rushed forward and thrust a knife deep into the ugly Sentinels armpit. She screamed and lost her grip on the sword. It clanged to the ground, masking the sound of her body falling.

Judging by the amount of blood she was losing, she wouldn't last long. Galan and Grog had warned Janu this would happen. She stared down at the soon to be lifeless body, unsure what to do. Should she help, even though it would be fruitless? The ugly Sentinel gurgled and mouthed something.

Galan and Grog were already at the other end of the hallway, yelling out to her. But the ugly Sentinel wasn't dead yet. She would die alone and cold if Janu didn't do something. Was there a blanket she could give her?

A new series of voices pulled her out from her confusion. The other Sentinels were in the hallway and on the stairs now, running toward her, Marrid and Ainsworth among them. Behind them she could see white daylight bleeding in through the open door.

Galan and Grog had left her behind.

DAMN IT! JANU would have made an excellent addition to the future Thieves' Guild. Imagine having the captain of the Sentinels, not the city-guard, the *Sentinels*, on your payroll. Every action against the guild, every patrol, every tip-off. They'd be unstoppable. *Legitimacy* might even be on the cards.

Just the thought of the Merchants' Guild having to sit at a council table with Grog and himself was too much. Galan laughed.

"What's so funny?" Grog asked as he darted past a stack of barrels in the alley.

Galan's boot sloshed through a puddle of muck. He tried to shake his leg as they ran. "I was just thinking about how —"

" —because of you, she's fucked back there, right?"

They took a turn out of the dark and into a bright side-street. A few people staggered back as Grog emerged and dumped into a cart, dislodging some turnips. Galan leapt the cascade of produce and caught up.

"She'll be fine, she's a Sentinel. They won't prosecute their own."

Grog scoffed. "You know as well as I that she'll be locked up for life. They don't tolerate corruption."

"Well, no. What's she done? Wrong place at the wrong time? They haven't got a case."

"You keep telling yourself that, mate. Keep telling yourself that they're not going to pin the whole thing on her and throw her down an oubliette."

What did Grog expect him to do? They couldn't go back now. There was no way into the Sentinel Headquarters to begin with, only the exit from the training yard. And they'd be securing that tighter than the Queen's own bedchamber now.

No. Janu was lost. And Grog was right, she'd probably rot in prison. But what could he do? It was hard enough keeping the two of them out of trouble, especially when one of them was a damned informant.

"Let's get back to the hideout," Galan said.

"Hideout? You mean that old shop? Janu's going to give us up in about five minutes after you left her back there."

"Hey! You're running along with me. I didn't see you try to do anything."

That seemed to shut him up.

"Besides," Galan said. "I don't think Janu will give us up. She's too smart. She knows that nothing she does will give her a lesser sentence."

The side-street ended at a junction with a main road. People streamed in both directions. Galan and Grog slowed their run and stepped into the anonymity of the crowds.

Grog looked down at Galan and lowered his voice. "When they put her on the rack, they'll get whatever they want out of her."

Why was he making such a big deal of this? "Not my problem." They'd lost many people to the Sentinels in Threerun, and Grog never made a peep back then.

They made the rest of their way to the shopfront in silence. As usual, the door wasn't locked. It was funny how much you could trust regular people.

Elvalor, Jendora, and Heather stood around the chair and table in the centre of the room. A smile came to Galan's lips at the sight, not of them, but that no one had dared to sit in his chair. Yes, the new Thieves' Guild was already on track.

"Funny seeing you three here," Galan announced. "We were just out looking for you."

"Well, when you didn't come to break us out, we had to improvise," Elvalor said.

Heather clasped her hands together. "He can play music!" she said.

"Yes, he's very good," Galan nodded. "Anyway, now that we're all out, we need to get out of here. The Sentinels might be looking for us."

"Don't worry, Galan," Jendora said. "They didn't interrogate us. None of us gave away this location."

Galan sighed as he took his seat. "It's not you three I'm worried about. They captured Janu."

"Why does that matter?" Elvalor held his hand to his chin and peered at Galan and Grog. "What did you two do?"

"Galan convinced Janu to betray the Sentinels and help us. In return, he left her behind in our failed attempt to break you three out of prison. He's going to let her take the fall."

Elvalor's mouth hung open. Jendora unfolded her arms and took a step back.

"No wonder the Thieves' Guild was so successful,"

Elvalor said. "You're planning things on a whole other level, Galan."

"That'll teach her to mess with us again," Jendora said.

Heather pursed her lips, glanced at Grog, and said nothing. Those two were getting too comfortable with each other, Galan would need to keep a watch on that.

"In any case," Galan said. "The party starts in a few hours, and we've still got to get ready. We're going to need some nicer clothes than these, and a few instruments to boot."

"Instruments? Like the one Elvalor played?" Heather asked.

"Yes."

"They're pretty expensive to get a hold of," Grog said, watching Heather. "We'll need a bit of money."

"That's alright," Elvalor said. "We've got two here, mine and the guard's one. We'll just steal the others."

"No," Galan said. "We're too close to the end now. Better not to draw any more attention. We'll buy them legit like. Grog, take Heather to get us some more instruments. Elvalor, go with Jendora to paint the horse white."

"What about you?" Grog asked.

"Me? I'm going to do what the leader of the Thieves' Guild does best. I'm going to—"

"—Nothing. The leader does nothing," Grog finished.

"*Plan*," Galan said. "I'm going to plan. I'm also going to find us a new place to lay low until tonight. This hideout is compromised."

A RESONATING WOODEN box with stretched lamb intestines was one thing, but there were so many other varieties of instruments. One was shaped like a bow but it was carved wood, not a supple limb pulled taunt, and with many drawstrings, each of which produced a different tone. There were oval shaped instruments like the ones she had seen before, and others that were like two circles touching and overlapping. Another instrument had the leathered skin of a pig stretched across a frame on the top of an open box, giving the strings an altogether different sound when plucked.

"We'll get one of each," Heather interrupted Grog and the shopkeeper.

Grog glanced back at her with a raised eyebrow. He lowered it, looking away. "She's a little slow, don't worry about her. We only need your three *cheapest* lutes."

"Surely you don't want your patrons complaining about the timbre of the music though?" The shopkeeper pulled down one of the 'lutes' that featured slivers of a calf's bones inlaid in a spiral pattern. He slipped his fingers across it, giving off notes that smoothed into being and wept into nothingness. Then he did the same to one of the cheap lutes. Its notes screeched into existence and screamed a long and painful death.

"We should get the nicer sounding ones," Heather said. "These other ones sound too much like the animals killed to make them."

"Unless you really do have a bag of platinum, we don't have the money." Grog pointed at the cheap lute the shopkeeper held. "Your three cheapest, please."

With a frown and slumped shoulders, the shopkeeper produced three lutes. They were made of pine, and had only a thin layer of boiled tree sap where the others had a thick, glowing coat. But, they were still instruments, and they were wonderful.

After exchanging a couple of gold coins, Heather and

Grog made their way out of the shop and back toward the market. The stalls were still open, despite the waning day, and people still milled about. They found a bench under a tree against the side of a closed blacksmith. Children ran past with screaming delight, something Heather couldn't ever remember doing.

"Can I see one?" She pointed at the lutes in his hands.

He shrugged. "Sure."

She pulled on a string and let it snap back from under her fingertip.

"Oh!" Heather smiled. *This is fun!*

As its sound faded away, she plucked another. They didn't quite sound right together. She tried the third string, it went well with the first. With two fingers she played both strings at the same time. It was magical!

"Try with your fingers up on this end." Elvalor and Jendora stood in front of the bench. "Press the strings down along the neck to make different notes."

He watched on as Heather tried. She was making the different sounds!

"Can you teach me?" she asked Elvalor. "To play like you?"

"No. Not like me. You're too old."

"We haven't got time for this," Jendora said. "Where's Galan?"

"Right here." Galan appeared from around the corner. "I got us a room at an inn. Good thing you got us paid in advance, Elvalor."

Grog leaned back and crossed his arms. "You know the Sentinels would have put the word out on us? There'd be an award."

"Not this guy." Galan smiled. "I promised him more

money than the Sentinels would ever pay him."

"It's always about money." Grog's tone made it unclear whether he was agreeing or not.

"Still." Galan stretched and motioned for Heather to shuffle over so he could sit. "Better we talk through things here instead of the room. Let's consider it a nice place to sleep, nothing more."

"So," Jendora said. "What's the plan?"

Galan scratched the stubble on his neck. "Thanks to Elvalor, we've got an in as a band of musicians—"

"—And now we've got these things!" Heather held the lute up.

"Yeah," Galan continued. "So we'll look the part. Once we're inside, all we need to do is find the unicorn." He turned to study Heather. "That's where you come in."

Though Heather wasn't sure she'd be able to feel the unicorn well-enough, she didn't want to say it might be a problem. Once they got her in, she had no intention of finding the damned thing anyway.

"Can do," she said.

"We'll need to deal with any guards watching it, Grog, that's you. We swap out the unicorn with the fake one, then lead the real one out through the catacombs."

Everyone sat in silence for a moment.

"How do we get the horse in?" Jendora asked.

Galan raised his eyebrows. "What's that?"

"How do we, as a music band, get the horse into the party, and through the castle to wherever the unicorn is?"

"Well... you see." Galan held a finger in the air. "Grog has a bag of hol—"

"—And what about the horn?" Elvalor asked. "It doesn't have a horn, it won't fool anyone."

"I… err," Galan stammered.

"And wouldn't missing guards get noticed? What if they have a patrol?" Grog added.

Everyone looked and waited on Galan. He began to mouth something but stopped.

Heather plucked away at the strings of her lute. She was getting the hang of this. "Why don't we just say it's a second unicorn, a party-gift for Radu?" she suggested. "They'd probably let us take it straight to wherever the real one is."

"That's exactly what I was going to say," Galan said. "But there is one other thing."

Everyone went quiet.

"In the cave, Jendora. Who was the dwarf with Janu?"

Jendora unfolded her arms and glanced at each person in the group before responding. "None of your damned business."

"No," Galan pressed. "If you're compromised, then it is our business. Who was the dwarf?"

She thrust her chin out. "A creditor. Marrid. I owe him money."

"How much are we talking about?" Elvalor asked. "Enough to be a problem?"

"No," Jendora said. "Marrid won't be a problem, he'll leave me alone."

Galan hopped off the seat and clapped his hands. "Right, let's go to the inn and lay low for a few hours until the party starts."

Heather followed behind, practising.

CHAPTER NINE

Escape Again

A COCKROACH SCURRIED across the damp stone of Janu's prison cell. Another emerged from a crack of mortar in the east corner and flitted around the window slit. With nothing but night outside it was dark, but thankfully some light from the guard's fireplace made it around the corner to her cell.

Not that there was much to see. Just bars, stone, bugs, and a bucket. Not even a bed. How many people had Janu put into a place like this? No, not people. *Criminals*, her adversaries. *They* deserved it. She never deserved it.

Janu sighed. This wasn't how it was supposed to happen. Siding with the thieves was only a temporary ruse, just enough help to get them going. Galan would've given up and never committed another crime if it wasn't for her intervention.

She *knew* she'd done the right thing.

Someone knocked on the door near the guard's post around the corner. Out of boredom more than curiosity, Janu got up off the floor and stuck as much of her face through the bars as she could. There was nothing to see but the fire-lit stone of the corridor.

Hinges creaked protest as the guard's door swung open.

A woman's voice spoke. "Good evening, Sentinel. Are you hungry?"

"Err, yes ma'am. But I—"

"—I'll just put this down over here then."

Sounds of crockery clinked around the corridor to Janu's ears.

The guard was quiet a moment. "Thank you, miss. But you really should go. No one is supposed to come down here without the Captain's order."

"That may be, but my job is to ensure that everyone has something to eat, by the Captain's order. So here I am."

"I don't recognise you." The guard spoke around a mouthful.

She laughed. "I'm new. It's my first night in the kitchen. I hope everything is to your liking?"

The guard murmured sounds of approval before speaking. "Yes." He swallowed. "It's very good, I don't recognise the taste."

"You might feel a little light-headed."

"Huh? What do you mean?"

"It's laced with mandrake," she said. "That's the unusual taste."

Sounds of chair legs scraping came around the corner.

"Am I going to die?" The guard sounded like a child.

The woman sounded like a mother. "No, you'll just sleep for a while. You'll be alright in the morning."

Was this how Galan did away with informants? It made a harsh sense; better to kill them than risk exposure. He was in for a surprise if he thought this would be enough to do her in. Is that why Grog has looked so terrible? Had Galan tried to caution Grog by poisoning him?

Footsteps proceeded down the corridor. Janu searched the room for something, *anything*, to use as a weapon. The bucket. *Eeww, no.* Death was better than that.

"So, you're the Captain Peter talks about so much in his letters."

A woman stepped into view. Her features hid her age well, though the lines in the corner of the eyes gave a hint. Nothing about her seemed interesting or remarkable, if anything, she was exactly what a woman who worked in the kitchen should look like. Overall, she appeared simple, the wife of a tradesman or skilled labourer. The perfect disguise for an assassin.

She dangled a ring of keys from her fingertips and started testing each in the lock.

"You won't find me easy to kill," Janu warned.

The woman raised one eyebrow. "I'm letting you out, I'm not trying to kill you."

"Who are you?"

The lock clanked. "Gwyn Ainsworth, Peter's mother. I'm breaking you out."

Of course! Ainsworth. That good head of his served him well.

"Thank you," Janu said. "Where is he? I need his help."

"He's not going to help you. You're no longer in the Sentinels. In fact from what I understand, you're now no better than a criminal. Worse even, you're the first Sentinel ever to go bad. He doesn't know I'm doing this."

It must have been Marrid then. "Marrid sent you?"

"The dwarf? No," she laughed. "He's even more upset than Peter."

"...I don't understand..."

"You're to be put to death for breaking your vow to the Sentinels and conspiring to kill the Queen. Though he doesn't know it, your betrayal has affected Peter deeply. As a test of his loyalty, he's to be your executioner." She swung the bars open. "I don't think he could do it. This way will be easier."

That ugly Sentinel must still be alive and put him up to it. Though harsh, it's probably exactly what Janu would ask for. If she were in the position to test someone's loyalty like that, she would never trust them again, not until the deed was done. Blood would prove loyalty. That was a lesson she learned on the streets.

"He'll never be trusted again," Janu said. "Not until he executes me."

"I know. But there is another way," Gwyn said. "If he and you put a stop to these criminals and bring them to justice, it could be argued that it was all a part of your plan."

"The Kalindar Captain would never believe it," Janu said.

Gwyn stepped aside and waved Janu through the doors. "No. But Radu will. And he holds more sway with the Queen than almost anyone."

"Are you saying the crown is under the thrall of a vampire?"

"Oh," Gwyn laughed. "Nothing like that of course. Just the wealthy are powerful and they all know each other. Far more powerful than even a Sentinel Captain. Money provides a power even magic can't surpass."

Janu had enough blockers put up every time she tried to investigate the well-to-do to know it was true. Orders would come down from above whenever she went sniffing around a well-connected merchant or lordly estate owner's son. She followed the woman around the corner.

"Where is Ainswor— Peter?"

"Why? I told you, he won't help you."

"But you said if we can stop—"

"—You're going to have to do that. And when you do, you're going to attribute the arrest to Peter. Once he sees that you never betrayed them, he will back you up."

"I can't arrest them alone, I need Peter and Marrid to help."

"Yes. Peter also tells me that there is a powerful druid to contend with?"

They stopped in the junction where the stairs led up to the headquarters, the doors to the training yard ahead, and the prison door behind them.

"Will you help me?" Janu searched Gwyn's face, but she was impossible to read.

"No, I cannot, at least not directly. But Peter has requested my help. He, Marrid, and I will be patrolling the party, the Kalindar Sentinel Captain has agreed to allow him that much freedom."

"The ugly Sentinel is alive?"

"...no. That one is dead. We're working with the *acting* Captain, the city hasn't appointed a new one yet."

Guilt swept like ice through Janu's thoughts. Now wasn't the time to think on it.

Gwyn unlocked the doors to the training yard.

Janu sighed. "Peter won't arrest the thieves unless they've committed a crime, will he?"

"No. They need to have the unicorn in their possession. It's *vital* the unicorn is taken from its garden before they're arrested."

Growing up on the streets forced you to learn a lot about

the way people spoke, how despite themselves, they revealed what mattered to them most.

"Why is this unicorn so important to you?"

"I want it." Gwyn seemed unsurprised. "A unicorn's horn has the power to restore life in the recently deceased."

Janu stepped backward and felt the cold stone behind her.

"Oh." Gwyn laughed. "It's not necromancy. With a well placed use of that power, I can climb through the noble ranks and join the Queen's court."

"I see."

"Though money buys many things in this city, a power such as that would buy me far more."

Helping Galan steal the unicorn out from Peter and Marrid's noses wasn't going to be easy. But she was trapped. Either be put to death by her own right-hand man, live a life on the run, or help steal a unicorn from a vampire.

"Do you know where I can find Galan and the other thieves?"

"I'm sorry." Gwyn opened the door. The yard was dark and quiet. "I haven't got a clue."

Janu stepped into the night. She felt for the reassurance of her sword, and remembered it had been taken off her, as well as her armour and money. It was cold.

She turned to ask Gwyn a question, but the woman was gone. A tingle of magic remained in the air.

GALAN SAT UPRIGHT on the bed, his back against the wall, flicking a knife around his knuckles in the warm afternoon sun. It streamed in from the open window, casting long shadows against the wall opposite. Muted sounds of pots and crockery came up through the wooden floor from the kitchen below. Faint sounds of coachmen calling out to their horses came in from the street. The thin walls did very little to silence the couple arguing two rooms over. Something about money and how the man had no love of work.

"How long now?" Galan stared at the light catching on the knife. He wasn't asking anyone in particular.

No one answered.

He let his head fall to the side. Grog was asleep on the floor, Heather was staring intently at a hole at the base of the wall. Elvalor and Jendora were still playing Riddish, but without any money to bet, it wasn't a very fun game.

"Hey," Galan said to Heather. "What are you looking at the wall for?"

"Hmm?" Heather rotated around. "Nothing. Just. Practising my magic."

"Do you practise often?" Grog asked with his eyes still closed.

Heather studied him a moment before replying. "Yeah... well. Nature is fickle sometimes. It makes it hard to know what to do."

Was that a hint of carefully chosen words he heard? "Any problems with your magic for tonight?" Galan asked her.

"No, no. Nothing like that. It should be fine."

Should be fine. Those were definitely some chosen words. He sat and thought about the situation, something he should have been doing all day. No Janu to guarantee safety, maybe no druid magic, a confused giant spider on the loose, and they were robbing a vampire. They were fucked.

"Grog," Galan got to his feet. It was time for the two of them to make an escape while they could. Let these other three keep at it if they wanted. "Let's you and me go for a walk, scope out what's happening."

"Huh? Why?" Grog furrowed his brow and opened his eyes. "No need for us to get spotted, it's not even dark yet. Dinner will be here soon anyway."

"Yeah," Jendora said. "No one's getting into the party until after sunset. Not even the cooks. Nothing is happening."

"I thought you'd have learned to be more patient than that," Elvalor said.

"Yeah. I just get antsy before a heist is all." Galan sat back down.

Fuck! He'd find a way to ditch them all later. Convincing Grog might be another problem altogether. He got back up and looked out the window, down into the inn's yard. Their 'white' horse was still down there, eating hay from a trough. The paint should be dry now.

A flicker of movement passed between two fence posts at the end of the yard. Galan narrowed his eyes. There it was again, a person, crouched down low. No one crouching down low in the shadows was up to any good, but what was a thief doing out there?

The door to their room opened. A slender boy, holding a laden tray entered, followed by a girl carrying two plates. They kept their eyes downcast and sat the plates on the table without a word before scurrying away.

There was nothing like a good tavern meal. Wherever you went, you could always get enough to eat at a good middle-of-the-road tavern. Galan had ordered the biggest meal they could afford. He always did his best thievery on a full stomach.

"Alright everyone, dig in." Galan grabbed a chicken wing and held a drumstick out for Grog.

"No thanks, I'll just have some of those potatoes and a bit

of bread."

That spider must have really done a number on him. "Still feeling a bit squeamish?"

"Huh?" Grog glanced up from his perusal of the food and averted his eyes. "Nah, I just… rather eat some veggies is all."

Whoever heard of an orc that didn't jump straight to whatever meat was available?

Heatherdown reached over and snatched an apple with one hand and a small dish of carrots. After watching her, Grog did the same.

Those two were becoming fast friends, though they tried to hide it. Galan went back to the window with his chicken, trying to use the glass as a mirror, intent on seeing what else Grog copied. But outside, on the other side of the yard, metal flashed in the light of the setting sun.

Those weren't thieves.

Galan took two steps back from the window, out of any potential arrow shot. "We're about to be raided," he announced.

Before he'd even finished speaking, Grog was grabbing a backpack and the lutes. Jendora and Elvalor seemed confused until Galan flicked a knife into his hand. They too grabbed what they needed.

Heatherdown stood, pocketing the apple, her meagre possessions already on her. "Raided? What does that mean?"

"The Sentinels are about to attack us." Grog stuffed lutes into the bag of holding.

"Attack us?" Heatherdown crouched like an animal. "Why?"

"Janu must have given us up." Elvalor tried to pin Galan with his gaze, but Galan wasn't having it.

"A hundred different things might have happened," Galan said. "Let's go out the front, into the street. We'll lose them in the crowd."

"Where do we go?" Jendora asked.

"To the party," Galan said. "There's nowhere left for us to hide."

Galan stopped for a moment. They were committing this crime, whether he wanted to or not. He shrugged and followed the others out the door.

The five of them pounded down the stairs, rattling the walls. A head poked out of a nearby doorway but disappeared at the sight of Grog's expression. Elvalor led them past the common room and to a side door that emptied them out into the street. Galan jogged to the front, and pulled Elvalor to a different direction.

"Let's head down this alley to the next street over," Galan said.

"What about the horse?" Jendora asked.

Shit! "We'll manage without it."

Elvalor slowed and pulled on Galan's sleeve. "You sure? Once we're in the party, if the alarm is sounded too soon we won't make it out."

Galan's heart skipped. "You're right. We should split up now. Call the whole thing off."

"Hold on," Grog said. "We don't need the horse. Even if they notice the unicorn gone, they won't be looking down in the catacombs. We're still on."

Damn him. He'd never been this dogged about a robbery before. They dashed through the alley and out onto the next road.

As Galan checked the flow of traffic, a burst of fire and sparks erupted against a nearby barrel, knocking it and several others over. A second explosion went off directly in front of Galan, stinging his face with flecks of dirt from the street.

He fell to his back, shielding his eyes with his forearms.

"Stop in the name of the Queen!" A man's voice yelled out from the alley behind them.

A second man's voice joined the first. "By order of the Sentinels, stop!"

Galan whirled around and watched a handful of Sentinels and city guards running down the alley. A plain-clothed woman stood at the mouth of it, her face more stern than even Galan's own mother. Beside her stood Jendora's dwarf, Marrid, and the Sentinel that always shadowed Janu... what was his name?

The plain-clothed woman wove her hands in an intricate pattern, leaving a trail of sparkling magic in their wake. It had been so long since Galan had seen a spell cast that he froze for a moment, gazing at the half-suspended filaments of power. Only when the fireball was hurtling toward him did he jump out of the way.

"Shit! Go go go!" he yelled at the others, pushing between them and making for the closest clump of bystanders he could see.

Angry shouts surrounded him as he forced his way through groups of people. A quick glance back showed the others close behind. There was no sign of more fireballs, but glimpses of armour near Elvalor highlighted a definite pursuit.

At the next crossroad, Galan paused. Both directions looked like main thoroughfares with about as many pedestrians for cover as each other. Why hadn't he spent time learning the city?

"Which way to Radu's?" he asked Grog.

Heather stepped up. "That way." She pointed.

A crack of thunder urged them all on faster. Who the hell was this woman slinging spells at them? Grog grabbed a cart and flung it behind them. They couldn't keep this up for much longer, even if they made it to Radu's, then what? Calmly walk in while being pursued by the Sentinels?

They needed something to force the Sentinels back, something to break off the pursuit. But there was nothing. Just people, shops, and carts.

"Lady Heatherdown?" Galan grabbed her by the arm as they ran. "We need a distraction. Cast a spell!"

She glanced back in concern. "What kind of spell? I only know nature spells, not shit like this!"

"Something to make the people panic!"

For a second it looked like she was going to argue, but then she closed her eyes and knitted her brow. Galan watched where she was running to make sure she wouldn't hit anything.

A woman screamed ahead of them, followed shortly by a man. Within seconds, people were running toward them, driven by an unknown panic. Sounds of fright and fear continued ahead of them, sending more people through their group and into their pursuers.

As they rounded a corner, Galan spotted the cause for the chaos. Legs was running around the street, jumping on stalls and people, skittering across horses and shops. At least he hoped it was Legs.

With no warning, Grog changed direction and scooped up both Galan and Lady Heatherdown. As he was twisted away, Galan caught sight of Elvalor and Jendora following closely behind. There didn't appear to be any sign of

Sentinels or stern, spell-slinging women.

Grog took them into an open door and crashed through the interior. He kicked out the door into the next street over. Their pace slowed despite the continuing chaos spreading in the street. Galan caught another glimpse of Legs as he climbed over the top of the building.

Heatherdown had her eyes open now.

"How far is it to Radu's?" Galan asked her.

"It's." She twisted and checked her surroundings. "One street over."

"We need somewhere to lay low," Elvalor said. "Just for an hour or so."

"Over there," Heatherdown said. "There's a cellar full of mushrooms that haven't been disturbed for a long time."

She wriggled free of Grog's arm and sprinted ahead. A steep set of stairs descended into a cavity under a stout, stone building. Grog descended the stairs in a single stride and shouldered the door open.

HEATHER CUPPED HER hand under a mushroom and tickled its spores into her palm. There were a few in here ready to send out clouds, but with the current population, any offspring would have a hard time taking root anywhere. They'd have a much easier time of it if she could help them, after all, it was the least she could do considering the intrusion.

It was supposed to be dark in the cellar, but Elvalor had insisted on lighting a lantern he'd found hanging by the door. Heather splashed through a puddle, over to the next bed of mushrooms and started teasing their spores out. She caught a glimpse of Jendora watching her, but nothing was said.

"We're fucked. We're so fucked." Elvalor paced the length of the cellar in three steps, turned and paced back.

Jendora turned away from Heather. "They're probably up there right now, knocking door to door," she said.

"We'll be fine." Galan ran his hand down one of the stone supports for the building above, investigated his fingers and wiped them clean on his trousers. "It's only for a few minutes now."

"That's plenty of time for them to find us." Grog stood by the wooden door, or at least what remained of it. Its old, weather weakened timbers didn't stand up well to his zeal when opening it to get off the street. "Where is Legs?"

Heather let her thoughts flow out like a web from the cellar. It felt different, like before, quiet, but there was Legs, having a great time.

"He's still around, but I think the guards are starting to close in on him."

"Better tell him to get somewhere safe," Grog said.

Elvalor whirled around. "Don't bring him here!"

"Oh god no," Heather said. "I'll tell him to hide up in a tree or something."

The message — well, more like a thought — back from Legs was that he was scared and hurt. Someone had managed to 'sting' him, which she assumed meant they cut him with something. She should probably tend the wound.

"I've got to go," she announced.

"Go?" Galan turned to face her. "You can't go."

"I've got to help Legs," she said. "He's hurt."

"Who gives a shit about a spider?" Galan said. "We don't have time, we'll be going to the party soon."

"Well..." If her plan succeeded, the fate of a spider wouldn't be her concern. Some other druid could deal with it. "Alright."

"How hurt?" Grog asked from the doorway.

"I don't know," Heather said. "He's a stupid spider. It could be a scratch, or it could be a missing limb."

Grog's mouth fell open, and a flash of anger passed over his face.

"They grow back!" she told him. "Invertebrates don't measure injuries the same as we do."

"Invertebrate?" Grog furrowed his brow.

"Boneless things," she told him.

He nodded and looked up to the ceiling, mouthing the word to himself.

"What's the plan now?" Jendora asked Galan. "Thanks to Grog, we've still got the instruments, but we don't have a horse."

"Are we going to steal another one?" Elvalor asked.

Jendora rolled her eyes. "Even if we did, we wouldn't find a white one, and we haven't got any paint handy."

"Can we do it without a decoy?" Elvalor turned to Galan.

"We can," Galan mused. "But it will be hard to explain why a troupe of musicians is wandering Radu's castle. It would be far easier if we had a unicorn to take straight to the other's stable... or wherever you keep one."

Heather rolled her eyes. That was her idea, not his.

"Is there time to paint us a new one?" Grog asked.

"No," Galan confirmed. "Our entry is as entertainment, we can't arrive late. But don't worry, we'll turn up with a unicorn yet."

"How are we going to do that?" Heather asked.

Galan pointed a finger at her. "You're going to shape-shift into one."

"I am?"

"Yes. Right now in fact. We've got to get to the doors soon. Is the coast clear, Grog?"

"Looks alright." Grog had the door open a crack, peering through.

"Great." Galan clapped his hands. "Let's get a move on. When we're up on the street, we'll find somewhere out of the way, and you can transform while no one is looking."

Everyone began gathering their things. Grog handed out lutes from the bag of holding.

"You want me to be a unicorn?" Heather hadn't ever really shape-shifted before today, not since she'd first been trained in how to do it. Nature didn't like it when druids did it at the best of times, let alone twice in a day. And what was worse, she hadn't planned to stick with the robbery after they got her inside, but now they wanted to take her the whole way.

"Yes, I want you to be a unicorn," Galan insisted. "Is there a problem?"

"No, no, problem."

The chaos in the street outside had all but dissipated. Snippets of conversation followed Heather as they walked toward the party, a werewolf was hunting people in the street, the spider was as big as a horse, Radu himself was stalking in the night for victims. Panic and the misinformation that bubbled up with it wasn't something she knew of from any other living creatures.

A line of city guards jogged past in heavy armour, their leader telling everyone in the street a many-legged creature was spotted digging in a garden four streets over. Everyone was to stay clear, get to safety and stay indoors. After exchanging worried glances, most of the people rushed away.

Legs was a block or so away, sitting in a tree, watching the guards walking by on patrol.

"I thought you said Legs was hiding in a tree?" Grog asked her.

"He is. There's nothing digging in a garden anywhere near here. These people are scared is all."

A woman ran by, clutching a wailing child.

"I don't think people were ever supposed to live in cities like this," Grog said. "They get carried away. I once heard a man in the slums cry out 'fire' for a laugh. Two people died in the stampede."

The city lost a little of its veneer in Heather's eyes. The once ingeniously gutter-lined streets syphoning excess water away were now clogged drains that kept stagnant, disease-ridden water accessible. The great walls of protective stone now seemed like a cage that kept the fear from evaporating. The orderly streets became a maze of confusion.

Heather sighed as the group rounded the corner. Ahead of them stood an open gate in the second wall of the city. The road, lit by two large bonfires and a hundred torches, went under the portcullis and straight to Count Radu's castle. It paled in comparison to the Queen's castle, and Galan had told her before that Count Radu lived in something called a 'mansion', but its tall stone and glass windows was a castle in her eyes.

Her castle if things went to plan.

"In here." Galan was off to the side of the road, beckoning the others over.

A little courtyard sat just against the inside of the wall, framed by the entryways of several closed businesses.

"Get behind these crates and do your thing," Galan said.

"Here? It's not..." The buildings surrounding the courtyard were tall, with many windows looking down. None of them were lit, but still... "I, um, I need a bit of privacy."

"Right," Galan said. "Of course. Ummm." He looked at the others and at the steady trickle of people walking by on the road. "We'll turn our backs, and sort of shield you from view. Is that okay?"

"Thanks," Heather said.

She walked behind the crates and glanced back. Everyone had done as Galan said, and were doing their best to shield her from a casual glance.

Okay. This is no problem. Just be a unicorn. Heather relaxed her barriers and let the natural world flow up from the ground and into her body. It wasn't the same as when she stood barefoot on the grass of her grove, but it was easier here in a dirt courtyard than it was against the stone of the prison.

Instead of the usual warmth of nature's magic, she felt cold. The earth was taking away her power, not granting her more.

No no not now. I need the power now more than ever.

A passing rat had stopped and sat on its hind legs, regarding her. It knew what was happening, probably heard about her transformation, and was having quite the laugh at her expense.

"Fuck off." She tried to shoo it away.

"Is everything alright?" Galan called back to her.

"Fine. Just. Give me a minute," she said.

Please.

Nothing.

"I... I can't," she said.

"What do you mean 'you can't'?" Galan came around the crates.

"I mean I can't transform. The natural world won't let

me."

Grog appeared around the crates. "*Let* you?"

"I can't just, *do* magic," Heather started to explain. "It's only possible if nature allows it. I fucked up in the prison and transformed into a rat. I wasn't supposed to."

"Why not?" Grog asked.

"Because it's against the rules, sort of. It's supposed to only be used as a last resort."

Galan spread his hands out wide. "Right, so you want to free the unicorn, and likely our only way to find the unicorn is if you transform into one so we can go straight to it."

"It doesn't work like that," Heather said. "I don't really know how it works."

"You don't know how your magic works?" Galan held his hand against his forehead.

"No one does. Druids just sort of have it, and it comes from the natural world. That's all I know."

Grog nodded and looked back at the others. They were all paying attention, but it wasn't clear how much they'd heard.

"Okay." Galan clapped his hands. "Change of plans. Elvalor, you're up."

"I can't transform into a unicorn," Elvalor said.

Galan ignored him. "Grog, hand out the lutes. We're a troupe, here to play some tunes for Count Radu's party."

"How are we going to get to the unicorn?" Jendora held her lute by its neck and studied the front of it.

"We'll improvise," Galan said.

CHAPTER TEN

At the Party

FIRELIGHT ILLUMINATED COUNT Radu's mansion so well that without the black sky behind it, one would think it was daylight. Every window of the three story extravagance was bright, every walkway was lined with braziers and torches. There were even parchment lanterns suspended on ropes between the trees.

It was a thief's worst nightmare. Galan turned back to the guard.

"We've travelled a long way to get here," Galan told him. "We only just arrived, we haven't had a chance to put our things down."

Elvalor stepped up beside Galan and began strumming his lute. "I was told we'd be given a room in the mansion in which to rest and store our equipment."

The guard squinted one eye as he studied the two of them. He glanced behind them. "You've only got a bunch of lutes."

"We're *the* lute orchestra," Elvalor said. "We use only

lutes and our bodies for percussion."

"Hold on," the guard said. "Mister Grant!"

A short, stocky man, dressed in finery, walked chin-first to them. "Yes, what do you want?"

"These blokes are supposed to be playing here tonight, but I don't remember hearing about them."

"We had all this sorted out the other day," Galan said. "Soladar hired us in Southport." That was the lie Elvalor had used before, wasn't it?

The guard crossed his arms. "I thought you said you just arrived."

"Yes, the rest of my troupe did," Elvalor explained. "I arrived ahead of them."

Mister Grant studied them down his nose and sniffed. "Who is Soladar?"

"One of Count Radu's aides," Galan said. Didn't these people communicate internally?

"Oh yes, Soladar." The guard nodded. "He's only new."

"I see," Mister Grant said. "Take them to the third floor east-wing. They will perform in the eastern garden." He surveyed Galan and the other thieves for a few moments, shaking his head. "Freshen yourselves up before you enter the garden, and please play only simple melodic tunes. This isn't a rowdy tavern."

With nods and noises of agreement they followed the guard into the mansion. He took them down a stone path that circled the front part of the building, away from the main entrance. It descended to an open staging area underneath the mansion, where crates, barrels, and carts sat lined against the walls. Plain-clothed men and women rushed about to the shouted orders of well-dressed, parchment-wielding foremen.

The guard entered a door and stepped up a narrow flight of stairs. The passage was dim, and didn't leave a lot of room if someone was coming the other way. Every so often the stone walls gave way to wooden panelling, only to become stone once again. Many doors and branching halls were ignored until they exited into a small room.

Red carpet softened underfoot as Galan entered. A tapestry depicting a musician before a seated audience hung from the opposite wall. Simple furniture sat against the walls; a table, chairs, and a lounge. There was no other finery or silver, the permanent staff had probably removed everything of value from the entertainment's rooms days prior. Count Radu mustn't be a complete idiot.

The guard closed the door behind them, the stonework attached to this side of it matched neatly to the wall. If Galan hadn't just entered through it, he wouldn't have known it was there.

"The door there," the guard said, pointing to the unhidden one opposite. "Will take you to a staircase. At the bottom, you'll find a hall open onto the gardens. You can set yourselves up on the stage out there. You start in a half-hour and play until everyone goes home."

"Thank you," Elvalor said.

"Alright everybody." Galan clapped his hands. "Let's get ready. Costumes first, then we'll tune!"

The guard wasted no time in leaving, closing the hidden door behind him again. Grog stepped up to the door and put his ear against it.

"Now what the fuck are we supposed to do?" Jendora asked. "We've got no fuck—"

"—don't worry about payment," Galan said overly loud. "We've got everything covered." He gave her an exaggerated nod and looked at Grog.

"Right," she said.

Grog gave a thumbs up.

"Okay," Galan said. Everyone turned to look at him. What the fuck were they supposed to do? They had no way to find the unicorn, and asking questions might arouse suspicion. And if they didn't play some decent music they'd be found out. "So... Elvalor."

"...yeah?"

"You're going to have to perform solo—"

"—nope. They're expecting a band, I can't be out there by myself."

"Okay, so go out there with umm...." Who did he need the least? The druid, despite having no magic, was the money. Only Jendora could get them out through the catacombs. He didn't want to leave Grog behind. "How many of us do you need to be a 'band'?"

"At least three of us."

"Shit, that many? Okay."

Galan looked at Grog. There may not be any loyalty left between them, but there was a lot of history. Who was he kidding? They'd never rebuild the Thieves' Guild, Grog would never be able to work in the city guard again, and with a secret family to feed... Galan's oldest friend wouldn't fuck him over, would he?

"Okay." Galan clapped his hands. "Jendora and I will go with you. Grog, you and Heatherdown are going to secure the unicorn and escape. The rest of us will meet you in Farrowood."

Galan's order was met by a chorus of objections. He held his hands out for calm.

"I have to go to lead the unicorn out of the caves,"

Jendora said.

"Grab a quill and parchment from Grog and draw him a map, quickly," Galan said.

"How do I know those two won't betray us and run off with the money?" Elvalor asked.

"You don't," Galan answered. "But I'm going with you, too. I'll vouch for them." Grog gave no reaction to that.

"I would like to play some music with Elvalor," Heatherdown said.

"What? No," Galan said. "You're going to handle the unicorn, and do what you can to help us find it."

Grog held a hand out. "How are we supposed to get through the catacombs and caves without our gear? We can't exactly walk around here with it."

Galan sighed. "Just grab whatever will fit in the bag of holding."

"I don't know how to play a lute," Jendora said. "Do you?"

"No. After you've drawn the map, Elvalor is going to give us a quick lesson."

"I can't teach you to play in ten minutes," Elvalor said. "We'll get found out!"

Galan clapped his hands for silence. Then he clapped them again. "We haven't got many options. This is it."

Jendora took Grog and Lady Heatherdown into a corner where she scrawled a map and explained it to them. Thank the gods these people knew who was in charge. Elvalor tossed Galan a lute and pulled him aside.

"Here. You just play these strings. Don't touch anything up here. When I say, you just play this string, then this string, like this" — Elvalor plucked the strings, one after the other, over and over again — "on each beat. That's all."

It looked easy. Galan had a go.

"You need to keep in time." Elvalor started clapping. "One, two, three, four, *one*, two, three, four."

That made it easier. He could keep time now.

"Okay, this isn't so hard," Galan said. "When do I stop?"

"When the song stops."

Jendora gave the map a final jab with her index finger then left Grog and Lady Heatherdown. Elvalor thrust a lute at her and got to work on her training. Galan stepped up to the table with the map, there was a series of lines scrawled on it along with copious notes at the edges. Grog was busy adding more.

"And she said if we get to a lake, we've gone too far." Lady Heatherdown watched what Grog was writing.

"Are you both set?" Galan asked them.

"No," Grog said. "You sure about this?"

"I don't see any other options. You two come down with us, but as soon as you see a chance, break off and search the grounds. The unicorn is probably in one of the walled gardens so it can't get out."

A knock ended all conversation. The normal, unhidden door swung inward. A halfling appeared, well-dressed, with the same superior attitude of Mr Grant. "You're expected on stage in five minutes. I suggest you make your way down there now."

Galan tried to clap his hands but found it difficult with a lute. "Right, let's get a move on... band. Time to go."

Shit. They were not ready for this.

GROG BUMPED INTO Heather at the top of the stairs. It wasn't his fault. She had never seen anything like the scene before her. For a start, the room was immaculate. Whoever had built it had taken sheets of marble and polished them so much they reflected like the surface of a still pond. From the ceiling hung iron chandeliers, bent and twisted to resemble hanging plants, but in place of each leaf was a candle. One wall had floor to ceiling doors, made from a series of small glass panels, framed by gathered lengths of fabric that she couldn't identify the animal source.

And then there were the people. A hundred. No, a *thousand* people mingled about in the room and spilled out onto the manicured garden beyond. Her cheeks felt hot as she gazed upon their clothing and then down at her own.

"Come on," Grog said in a voice for her ears alone. "Don't gape like an idiot. Look down there." He pointed to a spot in the room below.

A long table sat against the wall, laden with food. Some of it she recognised, a dead duck, a dead pig, a dead goose. Slivers of dead cows sat in a mound, surrounded by ripe fruits. Others she couldn't recognise the source of... but people were eating it all the same. What did it taste like?

"We should get some of that food," Heather agreed.

"What? No. The door."

She tore her eyes away from the food and watched a servant enter a door near it. As the door opened, she caught a glimpse of a large room beyond.

"A kitchen for a party like this would be very busy," Grog said. "Easy for us to slip into unchallenged and then slip away."

"Would they have more of that food in the kitchen?" Heather asked.

"...Yes."

"Then we should go."

They descended the stairs behind the others.

Conversation died down and a hundred faces watched as their troop entered. Grog bent his knees as he walked and ducked his head down.

"They don't see too many orcish people on this side of the walls," Grog said to her. "We might need a bit of a distraction before we can get through that door unnoticed."

The crowd parted once they got to the bottom of the stairs. Conversation sparked up again as they made their way to the garden beyond the doors. Women, eyes painted with various colours, looked Heather up and down as she passed them. Some of them sneered and turned away, others stifled laughter, and still a few openly laughed and tugged on the arms of others to see. Heather's face burned, and she kept her eyes firmly on the carpet.

Outside, the looks and laughter didn't stop, but with the additional space it didn't feel so much like walking through a corridor of faces. Elvalor jogged ahead and leapt up to a raised wooden platform that sat between two columnar trees against a tall wall. The trees were in distress because the stage was made from the timber of a fellow columnar that once stood between them. Despite all its grandeur and appeal, the civilised world was as brutal as the natural.

Elvalor gave a little bow and raised a hand, begging the audience to give him a chance to speak. They were all quiet, and no one apart from a stubby little man sitting at a nearby table was paying Elvalor any mind.

"Thank you. Thank you. Please, let us start the night with a solo performance. This song is called *Dragon Fire O'er the Gabled Roofs*.

As soon as the notes rang out, Heather was taken away to a mountain bristling with dragons in flight. A hand on her shoulder pulled her back.

"Come on." Grog flicked his eyes up at Elvalor on the dead columnar. "He's got their attention now, we can make a move."

"Don't forget." Galan appeared beside them, speaking in a harsh whisper. "Keep out of sight of the permanent staff. The two of you don't exactly look the part of hired help. When you find the unicorn, get it and get out of here. We'll meet you in Farrowood."

"Where do we meet?" Grog asked.

Galan's shoulders lifted a little, and his eyes glistened. He smiled.

"Don't worry," Heatherdown said. "The trees will tell us when they're in the wood."

"Let's go," Grog said.

He led the way along the edges of the garden, back toward the open doors. Wisteria cascaded over the top of the walls. She tried to ask the purple blooms about the wall, to find out what was on the other side, but it turned its flowers away from her and remained silent. Nature was being a real fickle bitch about her rat transformation.

Once inside again, Grog made a beeline for the food table. As they passed she couldn't resist reaching out to snatch one of the unrecognisable foods. It was some kind of a bread, she'd seen those before, but it was minuscule, and within it was some kind of... sugared milk. So sugared it was thick. It smelled of cinnamon and rich vanilla.

As Grog turned the door-handle and peeked inside, she took a bite. It was incredible. She'd eaten bread before, but this was different. It was full of air and didn't have any of the little bits of ground-up stone the usual bread had. And it was as sweet as a fruit! The inside sugar-milk was thick and smooth, it slid around her tongue.

Grog opened the door and went in, she followed.

People flowed about the kitchen in an uncoordinated mess. Women in white aprons carried metal pots of boiling foods away from stoves. Hips bumped and voices yelped as contents sloshed over the sides of trays. Others tried moving around each other but stepped in the same direction, making sounds of frustration before continuing on. A fire flared up from the back. Someone screamed and cursed.

"Come on," Grog said. "This way."

A narrow staircase, much like the one they entered the mansion via, took them away from the chaos of the kitchen and into the relative quiet and orderly spaces between the walls. There must have been as much space between the rooms and hallways as there were rooms and hallways. Why did they exert so much effort to ensure that the workers who brought the food and cleaned the mess couldn't be seen?

That would all change once Heather took control. She just needed to find Radu first.

Grog stopped in a widened area where four of the narrow passages met. "Do you have any idea which direction the unicorn is?" he asked.

"No... well. Hold on." Heather relaxed and tried to will the magic from the floors and walls connected to the earth, from the air circulating outside. It was still denied to her. "I'm sorry. I... I think I have to make amends before the magic will return?"

"Make amends?"

"I need to do something to benefit nature of equal proportion to what I took away."

His eyebrows went up, and his head cocked to the side. "I don't understand, what did you take?"

Heather sighed. "Transforming into another creature is

borderline unnatural. A druid's magic comes directly from nature itself, so it is only in the druid's power so long as it's nature's will."

He nodded his understanding.

"When I transformed into a rat," Heather continued. "I took energy out of the system. That energy could've been needed by a chick to crack through its shell, or for a rain to fall, or for an eagle to kill a mouse."

"So now you need to give back to that system you took from?"

"Yes."

"How do you do that?"

"A thousand different ways. I could plant a tree... or maybe a hundred. Remove an invasive species from an area, or—"

" —free a unicorn?"

"Or free a unicorn." It wasn't what she was here to do. But maybe all things considered, she should? One less thing for the druidic council to be upset about.

"Well." Grog scratched at the stubble on his cheek. "Let's find a room with a window. If we're lucky, one will look out on a garden. If Galan was right, we might find the unicorn down on one of the lawns."

The first room they entered looked very much like the one their gear was stored in. Lush red carpet lined the floor, a small table sat in a corner, and two paintings hung on the wall. The window looked out onto an open space, more stone than garden, with a man-made pond in the centre. Stunted trees, angry at their lack of root space, sat around the pond complaining to the large goldfishes that swam in it. Without enough space, the two fish swam endless circles around themselves, complaining about each other's personality quirks.

Though Heather was pleased to be able to sense that much, there was no unicorn, or talk of a unicorn.

Grog shook his head. They went back into the passageways and found another door.

A massive bed, larger than all the beds Heather had ever slept in, dominated the room. Cloth bags, bulging with duck feathers, covered the wool filled mattress. Layers of blankets sat in mounds and folded over each other. The entire length of one wall was occupied by a single, long painting, depicting more sexual acts than Heather had ever contemplated, many of which seemed physically impossible, or at least uncomfortable.

On one of the small tables to the side of the room was a tall glass container, filled with a red fluid. Grog walked over to it.

"This must be Radu's chambers," he said, keeping his voice low. He lifted the glass stopper from the container and inhaled over it. "Just wine."

From the mass of bedding, something stirred. A thin, pale arm fell out of the blankets, dragging a torso along with it, then a head. From nearby, a leg stretched toward the ceiling and flopped down. Long black hair fell across a man's pointed face as he sat up and rubbed his eyes.

He yawned and saw them. A frown pulled at his gaunt features. "I thought I told you people not to disturb me until midnight."

"Who are you?" Heather felt around in her satchel for the oak stake.

"Count Radu, of course." He sluiced his hair away from his face. "Are you here for the party?"

"No," she said, pulling the stake and pointing it at him.

"I'm here for you."

GALAN PLUCKED AWAY. *One*, two, three, four, *one*, two, three, four...

This was easy.

One *and* two, three, four! Did Elvalor hear that extra note?! Why didn't he mention you could slip extra notes in there? It might not be a bad idea to keep this lute and practice after all this was done. If the guild didn't work out a second time, maybe Galan could take up music with Elvalor.

Of course, they'd have to have a conversation about who would be the front-man.

One, two, three, fooooouuuuur.

Though there was no applause, Elvalor took a deep bow. Galan bowed and then followed Elvalor off the stage with Jendora close behind.

Elvalor turned and pulled them both to the side next to one of the skinny trees. "I don't know how much longer we can keep this up. I'm running out of songs in C-Major."

"We can't play all night?" Galan asked. "If they find the unicorn missing—"

"—when. *When* they find it missing," Jendora said.

"When they find it missing, if we've done a runner, Radu will come after us first."

Jendora leaned in. "Then let's just go *now*."

"We can't," Galan said. "Grog and Heatherdown need as much time as we can give them to find the unicorn. If we leave early and they come looking for us, they might find Grog and Heatherdown. At least while we're here, they have the cover of saying they got lost on their way to the privy."

"Privy?" Jendora furrowed her brow.

"Toilet," Elvalor said. "Fancy word for shitter." He shook

his head. "What are we supposed to do then? Not only is this music giving me a bad name, but a few of the patrons have been giving us sideways glances. Who ever heard of a band of just lutes, with two very obviously amateur musicians?"

"I don't think we're that bad," Galan said.

"We're trying our best," Jendora added.

Elvalor stood upright and held his palms out to them. "I'm sorry. I know. You're both trying your best. But these people expect more..." He leaned back in again, his tone dark. "And if my name gets around here and ruins my future prospects, I expect you to increase my share."

There it was again. Elvalor's irreverent personality was revealing itself to be an act masking his true nature. He would be a good asset to the new Thieves' Guild, if he could be controlled.

"There's enough money in this heist that none of us will ever need to work again," Galan said. "*If* Grog and Heatherdown find the unicorn and get it out of here." He fluttered his arms to stop the incoming arguments. "And so long as we don't arouse suspicion upon ourselves. We could be followed to Farrowood, or scryed from afar, you know?"

"Someone like Radu probably has a team of wizards on retainer for things like that," Jendora nodded.

"I don't give a shit," Elvalor said. "I'm out of here. You needed me to talk you into the party. I did that. I know you're having a hard time of it, so I'll only take seventy-five percent of what I'm owed."

"We haven't got that money," Galan said. "Just stay and wait. You'll be walking away from a fortune."

Elvalor spoke beyond a whisper. "Pay up now, or I start telling stories on my way out of—"

"—Galan Leafwhisper. Elvalor. Fancy seeing you two

here," a familiar voice said.

Galan turned, cringing at the realisation that someone knew who they were. Lady Vars stood next to the stage, dressed far more elegantly than she had in the Black Dog Tavern. She held a slender copper cup in one hand and a cloth-wrapped pastry in the other. Standing a few metres behind her were Messrs Vars, engaged in conversation with a small group of people. A smile played about on her face.

"Galan I didn't know you were a musician, I may have played cards differently had I known that."

Shit. What could he do? There wasn't any point in denying who they were. "Good evening Lady Vars. *Elvalor* and I were just discussing what song we should play next." At least with his name out, Elvalor might now think twice about ditching them all. "Do you have any song requests?"

"No." Lady Vars laughed as though she just won a hand of Riddish. "But I have a request of another sort."

Elvalor's demeanour switched back. "What's that?"

"Cut me in on your unicorn theft."

"Who the fuck is this?" Jendora threw up her hands.

"A friend, dear," Lady Vars said. "For a price, of course."

"I thought you were in the prostitution business?" Galan asked.

"No, no." Lady Vars looked hurt, but then shrugged. "Not unless he or she is of a particularly curious people. I once had someone request a formian soldier cast for... nevermind. No. I deal in exotic goods."

"Like a unicorn?" Elvalor asked.

"Yes. Whoever your buyer is, I'll pay double."

"Our buyer has very deep pockets," Galan said.

"Mine are deeper. I would have purchased it from Radu had he not grown so attached to it."

How could Galan swing this? As it stood, he wouldn't even *see* the unicorn; no doubt Heatherdown would release it as soon as she was in Farrowood.

"I'm sorry Lady Vars," Galan said. "Things are already in motion, I'm afraid you're too late."

"I'm sure you will find a way," Lady Vars said. "If you don't, I will alert Radu and the guards to your presence and your intentions."

"You pretentious bitch!" Jendora looked ready to start swinging fists.

Elvalor grabbed her.

"Bring the unicorn to the eastern side of the valley as soon as you can. I will wait there for the next two days with your payment. I'm sure you understand what life will be like for you if every guard from here to the Guiding Tower is looking for you."

At least she was giving them some leeway, or maybe she didn't know they were stealing it tonight. Where was she getting her information from anyway? Just how many people had Grog betrayed them too?

"How did you... know?" Galan asked.

"I knew who you were the moment you sat at the card table. Seeing you here now, it's not hard to put two and two together. Your faces when I mentioned the unicorn confirmed it all."

Damn it.

"So, do we have a deal?" Lady Vars asked.

"It's a deal" Galan smiled.

After she stepped away and joined the conversation with her sons, Galan dropped the smile and grabbed Elvalor.

"You need to keep performing by yourself. Jendora and I are going to go looking for Grog and Heatherdown to tell them what's happened. If they disappear into the catacombs with that unicorn we're never going to see it again, and then we're fucked."

"They're expecting a band, not a solo artist," Elvalor said. "They're going to start asking questions."

"If they do, tell them we're resting because Lady Vars requested you play solo." Galan glanced at her back as she laughed at some witticism. "She'll play along with that."

"Which way do we go?" Jendora asked.

"I think I saw them go into the kitchen," Elvalor said.

"Alright." Galan clapped his hands. "Let's go."

CHAPTER ELEVEN

Janu Comes Back

WITHOUT THE SENTINEL insignia, people didn't treat a gnome with much respect. Granted, the people of Kalindar didn't treat each *other* with much respect, but that was mild indifference. When they looked at Janu and continued walking directly through her path, it felt hostile. With so much time passing since she experienced it last, the sting of it didn't fade so easily.

Radu's party guests queued for entry from the mansion, down through the inner wall, and into the city. On the city side of the wall, eager tavern keepers and merchants wheeled carts up and down the line, selling overpriced refreshments and food. By the look of it, the city guard was out in full force, keeping the line moving and keeping the riff-raff from bothering the well-off too much.

At the gate, a wall of guards stood shoulder to shoulder with interlocked tower-shields. From between the gaps a further row of guards with crossbows stood several metres behind. Each carriage was inspected, every compartment opened, and then every individual questioned. Dirty children, excited by all the activity, ran up to the wall of steel. Metal boots kicked them away.

Janu frowned. The city guard was taking this job seriously. But there was always a way into anywhere for a desperate criminal. She closed her eyes and tried to recall the details of some of Galan's more impossible thefts, or even the old lessons she learned as a child.

She followed the wall around until she found what she was looking for. An arch shaped hole at street level, spilling a trickle of muck into the gutter. In a gnomish city, the drains and gutters were covered or hidden inside the construction; humans could build big, they just didn't think of all the details. No different to the city guard.

Metal bars, set into the stone, covered the hole, but time and water had worn into the mortar and rusted the bars. She checked her surroundings to be sure no one was looking, picked up a rock, and cracked it against the iron. After a few hits, she stopped and waited. When no one came to investigate, she got to work again, eventually loosening one enough to break off.

The outlet was narrow, but the stone was slick, allowing her to squirm through without much difficulty. Ahead there would be somewhere to break through, at least she hoped so. Going backwards would be almost impossible.

But then what? Even before crawling through this filth, there was no way she was going to be able to walk freely in the mansion. She'd have to find new clothes, something gaudy enough to look like a guest at a glance. Finding the unicorn was going to be hard as well, especially if Galan had already taken off with it.

She crawled as fast as she could until a light appeared

ahead. The top of the drain opened up, but was covered by bars of metal. Rolling onto her back showed nothing but firelight and bushes. Distant music drifted over her.

There wasn't a lot of give in the bars. She tried her feet. A splinter of stone cracked away. Janu squared her shoulders, set her feet against the bars and pushed. One of them shifted. More flecks fell.

"Who's there?" a voice called out.

Something shuffled in the bushes over the drain.

"Hello." The voice was a man's. The cadence of each syllable was off; maybe a foreigner. "Hello!"

Janu stayed completely silent. The shuffling moved away. Relief flooded through her. The voice mumbled something as it left.

After another few minutes, she tried the bars again. A larger chunk of rock fell, releasing two of the bars. Janu sat up and crept out of the drain.

Tall, thick bushes surrounded her. Behind her, a wall. In front of her, between the bushes, were glimpses of trimmed grass and neat flowerbeds. The distant party could be heard over the wall behind her.

She peered through the leaves in the direction the voice had gone. Nothing.

Standing slightly, she looked over the top of the bushes. It was a large garden space, encased in a tall stone wall on three sides and against the mansion on the fourth. She was in the corner, nestled between two tall, slender trees. Diagonally across from her, next to the mansion, stood a white horse. Dark windows high on the mansion wall overlooked the garden, beneath them was a single, closed door.

"Hey! Hey! Who are you! What are you doing here!" The

same voice from before called out from the mansion, but Janu couldn't see where they were.

The horse trotted over.

"Hey! You're not supposed to be here are you? Oh! Are you from the party! Do you have any molasses?"

Why did that horse have a horn on its— *oooooooohhh*. The unicorn stood before her, its head held up in pride. Starlight glowed off its white coat, giving it an ethereal aura that caught Janu's breath. Up close, the movement of its muscles were obvious, it was a powerful creature. A faint rainbow of magic glimmered from its horn as though the light was always caught at just the right angle.

"He*lllooo*, are you okay? Do you have any molasses?"

Did... did it just talk to her? Its lips moved...

"Umm...," Janu said. "No. I don't have any molasses."

"That's a shame. Are you from the party? Do they have molasses there? Can you go back into the — *eww* by the way — sewer and bring me some? But maybe *don't* bring it back from the sewer, and *instead*, bring it back through the door over there." The unicorn turned and pointed with its muzzle.

"No. No, I'm not from the party."

"Oh." The unicorn's head drooped. "Well... thanks anyway. I'll... just go back over there and wait. Maybe they'll bring some molasses in a little while."

The unicorn walked back across the grass, weaving around a flowerbed as it did so.

She'd found it! A smile of relief flooded her face as she made her way toward the creature. The other side of the garden was much like the former side. Stones lined a bed of low, thick-leafed plants. She dusted off a rock, sat down, and studied the unicorn.

"What is it? Is it a spider? Oh *gawd* I hate spiders," the

unicorn said.

"No. There's no spider. I'm just...." Janu sighed. "I'm just really happy I found you."

"You are? Why? Why are you happy? Why were you looking for me? Who are you? Do I know you?" The unicorn put its muzzle very close to Janu and snorted.

"I am Senti— I am Janu. I've been looking for you because someone is going to steal you and I want to arrest them."

"*Steal me!* Oh no. Oh *no*." The unicorn spun away. "Oh gawd, criminals. That's how I wound up stuck here."

"Stuck?"

"You're going to want to sit down to—" The unicorn spun to face her. "So this guy comes into my forest. He's big and ugly and very smelly. Stomps around for a bit, dragging this other guy behind him."

"Right."

"And so this other guy is thin and young, like hardly even grown, just a little sprout. So I come up to them in a clearing, and I ask them, 'hey what's going on?', and this guy throws the kid to the ground in front of me and says 'here's a virgin'."

"A virgin?"

The unicorn shook its head. "Don't get me started. For some reason everyone has it in their head that I'm some kind of pervert. Maybe that's why they locked me up in here, but I swear I never touched the kid."

Janu looked at the door. It was still closed. "So what happened?" she asked.

"Weeellll. Long story short, they caught me in a net. The big guy was being followed by some other big guys who were invisible."

"Invisible?"

"*Yes*. Magic oohh." The unicorn paused and brought one eye down close to her. "You *do* know about magic don't you?"

"Yes. I'm a gnome."

"Great. So anyway, they tied me up and carted me away in a wagon and I ended up here."

Janu wasn't sure what to say.

"And now *more* criminals are coming. At least they feed me here. They have molasses sometimes. You said you didn't have any molasses didn't you? Forget it, I already asked you that didn't I?"

"Yes, I don't." Janu thought about what she said then shook her head. "The criminals are coming to steal you and release you."

"Release me? Back into the forest...." The unicorn pranced around for a moment then came to a stop. "There isn't any molasses in the forest. They sometimes have molasses here. I think I'll wait and see if there's more."

"I'm not going to let them steal you," Janu said. "You'll be fine here."

"Great."

By the sound of it, the party was still going full swing.

"How umm... How often do they bring you molasses?" Janu asked.

"Oh um, once."

"A day?"

"No. Once. They gave me some once. Since then I just have a little nibble on the grass here when I'm hungry."

"I see."

"Are you going to stay here?" The unicorn asked.

"Until the criminals come."

"Okay... but you can't have any of the molasses."

"No problem. I don't think I like molasses."

The unicorn whipped its head. "Good. But what's wrong with you?"

Where was Galan? Hopefully he'd get here soon.

How any of the servants managed to navigate about Radu's mansion was beyond Galan. Passages splintered off in every direction, each of them sharing the same undecorated stone punctuated by the occasional lantern. You'd think they'd leave some directions on the walls or at the junctions.

Galan stepped right, then shifted to the left instead. The right-hand passage looked too dark. He stopped at a door, and eased it open slightly. An empty bedroom. There was nothing but a wall of scrolls and a cushioned seat in the next room.

This was taking too long. They couldn't search every room down every passage. All they needed was a way into the unicorn's garden. Assuming it was kept in a garden.

"The unicorn wouldn't be hidden away right?" He asked Jendora.

"No. A creature like that you'd want to show off. You'd want it to be easy to show others."

"Right, yes." Galan nodded and tapped the wall. "And it's like a horse, right? It needs an open space, lots of grass."

The front of the mansion, where they entered, didn't have anything like that. It was stone frontage all along the road.

"It must be in the back of the mansion," he said.

"Back the other way," Jendora said.

"Are you sure?"

"This is practically a man-made cave. I'm good with caves." Jendora pointed behind her. "The back of the mansion is down that other way."

Galan squeezed past and rushed forward. He ducked into the darker passage and jogged onward. Something crashed into him at the next junction, knocking him against the wall and spinning him to the ground. A cup bounced and came to rest in front of him.

"Keep to the left!" An angry woman shouted at him.

"Sorry," Galan muttered, rising to his feet.

She was an elderly woman, plump, definitely a servant. He grabbed some of the dropped cups and handed them to her.

"What are you about?" Anger still laced her tone.

Galan thought fast. "I, we, are on our way to... assist in feeding the unicorn."

"That bloody useless thing. You're the new handlers?" She looked them up and down. "Why are you all the way up here?"

"We got lost," Jendora said.

"You'd think they'd put some directions in this stupid place," the old woman said. "We're always getting lost in here." She sighed, the last of her temper evaporating. "Go down this way and take the second left. First set of stairs go all the way to the bottom." She stopped and mouthed something to herself. "Yeah. First set of stairs. Then go left and it's the third or fourth door on the right."

"Thank you," Galan said.

"I know what it's like to be new here," she said. "But you'd both better get going, I heard the Count is planning to show the beast off later tonight."

As they hurried down the passage, Jendora pulled back on Galan's sleeve.

"What are you doing?" she asked. "The second left is

here."

Behind her, another passageway branched off. It was dark. How did he miss it?

Jendora went ahead. "We should wait until after Radu is done with the unicorn before trying to get it out of here," she said.

"Let's just focus on stopping Grog and Heatherdown first."

"What are we going to do about her? The druid I mean. She won't be happy with the change in plans."

"I haven't thought that far." Galan stared down the passage ahead.

Jendora glanced back at him. "I can deal with her if you want."

He was hoping she'd handle it. Galan nodded.

They found the stairs. They were steep, closer to a ladder than a normal staircase. The stairwell seemed to penetrate the entire height of the mansion. Above them a lantern swung, someone was moving from a level above them to a level higher.

As they climbed down, Jendora spoke again. "How are we supposed to get the unicorn out of here?"

"Grog's got something for that," he said. "We planned for it."

She nodded.

At the bottom of the stairs, Jendora took off down the passage until they reached another junction. The passage continued on straight ahead, or to the right.

"She said left, didn't she?"

"Yeah, but she must have meant right."

The passage was lined with doors on both sides.

"Third or fourth on the right," Jendora said.

Galan tested the third, then fourth door. Both were simple rooms with plain wooden beds and no decoration. At a guess they were spare servant's quarters.

"This can't be right," he said. "There's no garden here."

"I think we're below the ground level anyway," Jendora said. "Unless the garden is recessed into the earth, we need to go back up a level."

"She *did* say all the way to the bottom, didn't she?"

"Maybe she just meant to the ground-floor, the 'bottom'?"

They retraced their steps. Galan looked down the passage leading away from the stairs.

"Maybe she really *did* mean the left? Down here?"

Jendora shrugged but followed.

The third door opened out onto a lit garden. Galan stepped through and noted the tall walls surrounding the grass and scattered flowerbeds.

"The criminals are here, the criminals are here!"

Galan whirled around to see a unicorn bucking and jumping.

"Help me Janu! They're going to free me!"

HEATHER PULLED THE knot of twisted sheets tight and stepped back from the bedpost. There was no way Radu was going to work his way out of that. Behind her, Grog stood next to the door — the normal door, not the hidden servant door — ready to prevent any intrusion.

Radu strained his wrists against the makeshift rope. "Please, whatever you want, just let me go and we can discuss it."

Heather yelled at him. "Shut up!" She needed him scared, animals — and people — made rash decisions out of fear.

"What do you want?" He tried looking over his shoulder at her, but she remained positioned where he couldn't get a good look at her.

"What *do* we want?" Grog asked.

When she'd first set out from the grove, she never intended to find the unicorn. But after Grog kept her lack of money secret, she hoped to be able to repay him. If they'd found the unicorn, she could have sent him off with it and directions to the druidic council. They almost certainly would have wanted him to join after freeing such an endangered creature.

But they found Radu first. Maybe it was for the best?

"What I want, is to kill this vampire!" Still behind Radu, she thrust the stake past his ear so he could get a good look at it.

"No! Please! Don't kill me!"

"Why shouldn't I? You're a horrible, evil, despicable, *unnatural* abomination. You must be put to death!"

"Wait! Money! I can pay you. Anything you want."

Grog pushed himself off the wall. "How about a unicorn and safe passage?"

Maybe she *could* still pay Grog back.

"Yes! Give us the unicorn, and I won't kill you." She was, of course, definitely going to kill him. But not until she got what she came here for.

"Okay! You can have it, but please treat it well. I love it so."

"And safe passage?" Grog asked.

"Yes! I promise, I won't tell anyone. No. I—I will tell them you're dear friends and to assist you as far as you want to go."

Grog walked around the bed, crossed his arms, and

looked down at Radu. "What kind of assurances will we have?"

"I—I—I don't know how... what do you need? Name it." Radu seemed to be getting a grip on himself.

That was no good.

"Yaaahhh!" Heather leapt over the bed and drove the stake into Radu's eye. White liquid burst and squished out around the wood.

Radu screamed and bucked against the restraints, waving the stake in the air.

"What the fuck?" Grog took a step back, uncrossing his arms.

"Are you scared!" She screamed into Radu's face then thrust her wrist into his mouth.

The screams muffled and Radu tried to turn his head away. She followed it, holding her arm between his teeth.

Come on, come on. Why wasn't he biting?

Grog grabbed her shoulder and tried pulling her back. She jabbed an elbow back at him.

"Get back!" she said. "I don't know exactly what happens when I turn. I might not have full control for a moment. Don't be too close unless you want me to bite you."

The hidden servant door opened and an elderly woman walked in backwards, holding a tray. She came to an uncertain stop as she turned around.

"I'm sorry to interrupt your festivities, master," she said. "Forgive the intrusion."

Heather pulled the stake free from Radu's skull and pointed it at the woman. "Don't let her leave, grab her!"

Grog had the old woman by the arms before the reality of the scene had affected her. She tried to pull her arms free but soon stopped.

"Hold on," Grog said. "What's going on?"

"I am trying," Heather said. "To get this vampire to bite me."

"Why?"

"Because I am sick of being told what to do and living in a *fucking dirty forest with a spider.*"

Blood stained the side of Radu's face and most of his chest. Losing an eye wasn't such a big deal for many creatures, and he was a vampire, it would grow back. Well, it would if she wasn't about to kill him.

"Now bite!" She thrust her wrist to Radu's face again.

Radu's voice was broken between his ragged breaths. "I'm not a vampire."

GALAN WATCHED AS Janu appeared in front of the unicorn, making shushing noises.

"Calm down, calm down," she said. "It's alright."

She looked like shit. Literally. Mud and slime covered her from head to toe, no armour, no weapons. Come to think of it, she reminded Galan of an orphan picking pockets in the streets.

"What are you doing here, Janu?" Galan asked. "Who else is with you?"

The unicorn had stopped jumping around but was breathing heavily. Galan couldn't see anyone else.

"I've come to help, as agreed," Janu replied. "We had a deal."

"Yeah, we did." Wasn't she angry that he'd left her behind in the prison?

"Hello... Jendora, isn't it?" Janu said. "I've been working with your brother. Don't worry, he hasn't said much about you."

Brother? That must be the other dwarf. Jendora remained stoic. Galan hadn't forgotten what she said about owing the other dwarf money. No one on this heist was being entirely truthful.

It was time for business. Galan crossed his arms and studied the unicorn. The beast's flanks were rising high with each breath, its head thrust upward in agitation. That horn looked like a significant weapon if it wanted to use it. This would be a lot easier if Heatherdown was here to help control it; this thing was far too like a horse for Galan's comfort.

"Have you handled the guards?" Galan asked Janu.

"Not exactly. I escaped prison. They weren't about to listen to me and look the other way."

"Right... Where's your friend?"

"What friend?"

"Whoever else you brought in with you."

"He means me," the unicorn said.

The unicorn talks. Why didn't Heatherdown mention that?

"Hello," Galan waved his hand at it. "My name is Galan. What's yours?"

"Sunshine Sapphire Rose." The unicorn raised its head. Sparkles sprinkled down from the tip of the horn and faded from existence before they reached the base.

"Well, Sunshine, I am here with a drui—"

"Sunshine *Sapphire Rose*," the unicorn said. "My name is not *Sunshine,* that's what the sun does."

Bloody hell. "Okay, Sunshine Sapphire Rose. My apologies. We are here to free you."

Sunshine Sapphire Rose reared and kicked at the air perilously close to Galan's head. "No! They're going to free me! Help me, Janu!"

"It's okay, it's okay." Janu reached calming hands up to the beast. "They have some molasses."

"I do?" Galan scratched the back of his head.

"Why didn't you say?" Sunshine Sapphire Rose said. "Let's go to the molasses. Now. There's no need for us to be here if there is molasses somewhere else."

Galan caught Janu's eye and shook his head. What the hell was the unicorn talking about?

"Yes," Janu said. "These criminals and I are going to take you to molasses." She gave Galan exaggerated nods of her head.

"Yes... that's right," Galan said. "We have molasses. Outside. In the east."

"Is that where we're going?" Janu asked. "To the east?"

"Yes. We have a buyer there."

Janu studied him for a moment. "I thought you were freeing it for the druid."

He really needed to remember all the half-truths he was keeping. "Yes. The druid, Lady Heatherdown, is the buyer."

"So... what now?" Jendora had wandered off a little ways, gazing up at the walls and the mansion. "I don't think our friend here is going to fit through that door."

Galan glanced at the door and the unicorn. Jendora was right, there was no way the unicorn came through there.

"How did they get you in here?" he asked Sunshine Sapphire Rose.

"Well at first there wasn't that wall." Sunshine Sapphire Rose turned to point its horn at the far wall, opposite the mansion. "But then there *was* the wall. There were quite a few wizards involved, placing wards and protection spells in every which corner."

"So you can't leave?" Janu held her breath.

"No," Sunshine Sapphire Rose said. "It's to keep other people out. I can't jump the wall though."

Where was Grog and his bag of holding? There was no other way they were going to get the unicorn out of here.

"Alright, we need to find Grog and Heatherdown," Galan said. "We only have one bag of holding and Grog has it."

Jendora raised an eyebrow. "You're going to put the unicorn—"

"—Sunshine Sapphire Rose." The unicorn stamped a hoof with each syllable.

"Sorry," Jendora said. "You're going to put Sunshine Sapphire Rose into a bag of holding?"

"How else did you expect us to get it through the caves?" Galan asked.

"You were going to go out through the caves?" Janu cocked her head to the side. "The mansion has an entry to the catacombs, and from there to the north... we never would have looked that way. Not a bad plan."

"Thank you," Galan said. "But things have changed. We're now meeting with the buyer in the east."

"You keep using that word 'buyer'," Janu accused. "Why did the plans change?"

"...Flooding," Jendora said. "Too much rain, the cave system is impassable."

"How long until Grog gets here with the bag?" Janu asked.

"There's no telling," Galan said. "It might make more sense for one of us to go look for him."

Jendora shook her head. "I'm not going. How do I know you won't leave me high and dry like you left her?" She pointed at Janu.

Janu laughed. "Yeah, I'm not going either, Galan. I'm

staying right here with the unicorn so tha—"

"Sunshine Sapphire Rose," the unicorn said. "I did you the courtesy of remembering your name, Janu."

"Sorry. I'm staying with Sunshine Sapphire Rose the whole way."

If Grog and Heatherdown got here while Galan was out looking for them, there was no telling what they would do next. Jendora didn't care if their names were known in every kingdom, she could just disappear into the mountains. With Heatherdown and her money, she would be a much surer bet than the old bitch who threatened them. He couldn't risk leaving the unicorn either.

Galan dropped himself to one of the stones lining the flower bed. "Then I guess we're all just going to sit and wait here."

CHAPTER TWELVE

Not a Vampire

TEARS AND SNOT cut through the blood on Radu's face. "It was just a stupid rumour, but it stuck. I thought it sounded good, you know? So I didn't say anything."

"He made us all spread rumours and leave sheep blood out where his guests could see it," the old woman said. "He wanted people to think he was a vampire."

No! This was her way out. This was her way into the cushioned lap of civilised luxury.

"Bite me!" Heather thrust the stake under Radu's chin.

He bit down onto her wrist. His teeth didn't even press into her skin.

"Damn you!" She cracked the side of his head with the stake. "No! You *are* a vampire! Bite me!"

"Why are you so sure he's a vampire?" Grog asked. "He doesn't have pointy teeth or anything."

"Because the druidic council *said* he was a vampire and they're never wrong abou..." Was there anything the druidic council was *right* about?

Heather slumped to the carpeted floor. It was so much softer than even the thickest bed of grass or layer of moss. She couldn't go back to the grove, not after feeling something like this against her skin. Going back to overripe fruit and undercooked vegetables after tasting the food here, to the sounds of birds cawing and owls screeching after she'd heard such beautiful music...

"Are you alright?" Grog took a tentative step toward her.

If she had the ability to, she would have summoned a vine so thick and strong that it would tear this whole damn city apart. But nature was still ignoring her. That was fine, she was going to ignore it too.

"We're going to take your unicorn," Grog said to Radu. "If you come after us you're going to lose the other eye. Do you understand?"

Radu sobbed agreement.

"Where is the unicorn?" Grog asked.

"Out the window there," Radu said. "In the garden."

Grog strode past Heather and leaned over the bed-like nook below the window. "I see it," he said. "And the others are down there too. We should go."

What was the point? "No.... I'm just going to stay here and enjoy the carpet while I can."

"Don't we need to free the unicorn?"

"I don't care," Heather said. "It's just another stupid animal."

"We had an agreement." Grog turned from the window. "I don't say anything about the money, you introduce me to the druid council."

Something clanged on the ground next to Radu. From his hand rolled a silver orb.

"What's that?" Grog asked.

"There is no money," she said. "It was all lies. The druid council doesn't have any money."

"What?" Grog took a step toward her.

A thump of air burst from above the rolling orb, flapping the bed sheets and curtains. It was followed by a flash of radiance that threatened to blind anyone who looked too closely at it. But before Heather could look at it, it was gone, leaving in its place three figures.

Fire exploded from one of the silhouettes, toward Grog, and struck a bed post, blasting fragments of flaming wood through the room. They struck Grog in the chest and flung him through the window.

Radu screamed. One side of his face was alight. Heather looked down at her own body and found it encased in a protective layer of vines. They were blackened and smoked in places. She hadn't done that.

As she stood, something shifted underneath her, launching her to the window. She tried to catch the frame but fell through anyway, landing in a tangle of twigs and branches.

The three figures appeared in what was left of the window as the bough lowered her to the ground. A young human man, an old human woman, and the dwarf from the cave.

A HALF-ORC IS big. But when they fall into you from exploding windows twenty feet above, they *feel* even bigger. Janu tried to duck under Sunshine Sapphire Rose, but the unicorn's reflexes outmatched her own. Janu took the full brunt.

With no wind left in her lungs she couldn't yell at the orc to move, and with the weight of him pinning her down she couldn't hit him. Not that it would matter anyway, he was unconscious and her limbs didn't feel right when she tried to move them. Her ears weren't working either.

Above her, Galan flicked knives up at the new hole in the wall. He had better eyes than her, all she could see was smoke. But he didn't stop. How many knives did he carry?

The weight moved. Then it rolled off her and collapsed to the side. Jendora thrust a hand down to Janu.

"Come on!" Jendora sounded muffled and faint.

Janu took the proffered hand and pulled herself to her feet. They wobbled for a moment. After a final blade took flight, Galan glanced at her and then to the other side of the garden.

"Get the unicorn!" He was barely audible.

Where was it? Darkness pushed in on the edges of her vision. Something bright was moving over the grass, that must be it. She took off after it.

The air felt thick. Every step seemed to take too long. Her legs refused to move faster. Something behind her eyes splintered into fragments. Pain seared her thoughts.

She opened her eyes. Grass. When had she collapsed? Had she ever gotten up? Why did her family ever leave the village? How had she ended up in the gutters of Threerun?

A white hoof came down onto the grass. Janu tried to push herself up, but her strength had finally betrayed her. It was never really there. She always knew bluster and arrogance would only get her so far.

Something hot touched her back and sent tendrils of light through her veins. She gasped as they embraced her lungs, and cried out when one penetrated the spot behind her eyes. Sunshine Sapphire Rose looked down at her.

"Janu! Janu! It's time to get molasses!"

The unicorn worked its muzzle under her arm and Janu

held on. Sunshine Sapphire Rose pulled her upright though she didn't need the support anymore. Janu shook her head. Sound came back.

In front of them, Galan and Jendora pulled Grog across the grass, away from the mansion. They hadn't made much progress.

Beyond the thieves the smoke was clearing, revealing the extent of the damage. Almost the entire upper story wall had vanished, along with a portion of the roof. Jagged stone and timber stuck out at odd angles. A small section collapsed on itself and crumpled to the garden below.

Three figures stood in the haze upon the second story. There was no doubt who they were, but why act now? Galan hadn't stolen the unicorn yet.

A fireball shot out from one of them, Gwyn, and struck the ground just short of the fleeing thieves. Sparks flew through the air. Marrid leapt from the hole and landed roughly on the ground, but rose to his feet, battleaxe at the ready.

"Jendora! Give yourself up. It's time to come home!" Marrid stepped forward.

"We need to help them," Janu said to Sunshine Sapphire Rose. "Only they know where the molasses is."

The unicorn thundered toward the thieves without a word, leaving Janu behind. Galan and Jendora dropped Grog and scattered, but the unicorn stopped before it trampled them. It wasted no time in touching Grog with its horn.

With a flurry, Grog got to his feet, his head swivelled in every direction. "What the fuck's going on?" he bellowed.

Galan reappeared just as Janu caught up. "Grog, tell me you have the bag of holding."

"I have the bag of holding." He still didn't look like he

knew what was happening.

"Get it out," Galan said to Grog. He turned to Sunshine Sapphire Rose. "Get in the bag."

Sunshine Sapphire Rose threw its head up. "What?"

"It's the only way we can get you out." Galan urged.

Marrid called out from the base of the mansion. "You're under arrest for the attempted murder of Count Radu!"

"Surrender, all of you!" Ainsworth's good head wasn't thinking well, he was still standing in the broken window, and besides the three of them were outnumbered. The criminals hadn't even taken the unicorn yet!

Another explosion of sparks hit the ground. Maybe Gwyn was aiming to miss?

"Marrid. Enough! I won't go back!" Jendora shouted defiance.

"Go fuck yourselves!" Galan added.

He loosed more knives, overhand, at the three figures. As the blades neared them, a burst of green from below shot up, deflecting them. Vines sprouted and intertwined, becoming thicker as more offshoots sprung out. Marrid and Ainsworth's mouths hung open as the foliage closed and blocked them from view. In only seconds, everything twisted and writhed until a solid wall was formed.

"He wasn't a vampire." The woman must be the druid. Who else would be dressed like that? And where the hell had she come from?

"What the fuck was that about?" Grog thundered. He held a sack made from coarse cloth in his fist.

Galan pulled it out of Grog's hand, unfurled and held it open. "Get in," he said to the unicorn. "We're getting you out of here."

"I'm not getting in the bag," Sunshine Sapphire Rose said.

"That's ridiculous."

"There's molasses in it," Janu said.

The unicorn thrust its head into the bag. As it did, the edges of the cloth expanded and flopped to the ground. Galan lifted the bag and pulled it over the beast's back, then gathered the edges and pulled. He held up the bag, back to its original size.

Grog snatched it from him. "I'll hold onto that."

"What now?" Janu asked. She hadn't meant it as a question to the thieves, it was a question for herself. Now was the time to arrest them, they had possession, but there were too many of them, and only one of her. Why had Ainsworth and the others revealed themselves so soon? An attempted murder charge? Galan wasn't even in the same room as Radu, it would never hold up in court.

"We get the fuck out of here." Jendora swung a hooked rope over her head and tossed it up the wall. It clanked on the far side as she pulled back. Then she was climbing it. "Come on. We need to hurry."

Galan and Grog followed without hesitation.

"You still owe me," Grog said over his shoulder.

Heatherdown sighed, grabbed onto the rope, and used it to walk up the wall.

Without any other options, Janu did the same.

Radu's mansion was as large as the centre of Threerun, or at least it felt like it. Every corner revealed another passage, every doorway led to a room with another hallway beyond. Galan smiled and nodded to the many heads that turned as he passed. Murmurs and gasps of astonishment flowed around.

"Where are we going?" Janu whispered to him.

"I'm looking for a way out," Galan said between his teeth. "Just smile and keep walking like we're just a part of the entertainment."

Guards rushed down a corridor in front of them, drawing the attention of many of the guests. An elderly man watched Galan out of the corner of his eye. After stopping at a hidden door — easier to find when you knew what to look for — Galan opened it and urged everyone inside.

"Why hasn't an alarm sounded?" Jendora asked as the door closed. "There was an explosion."

"These people probably thought it was a part of a show or something," Grog said.

"Marrid and Ainsworth will be looking for us," Janu said. "They'll shut the party down and flush us out."

"Same tactics you used to clear out Threerun," Galan said.

Janu studied him. "Effective."

Heatherdown stared down the semi-lit corridor.

"Can you use your magic to get us out?" Galan asked the back of her head.

She didn't seem to hear.

"Hey! Lady Heatherdown."

"Huh?" She turned, eyes flicking across the faces watching her. "Wha—no. I didn't do that vine wall."

"*You* didn't?" Grog pulled at his ear. "Who did then?"

"That woman with Marrid." Jendora pulled the door closed. "She was slinging fireballs at us."

"No," Grog said. "Wrong kind of magic, I think. The vines were nature magic."

Galan clapped his hands. "It doesn't matter. We need to get out of here before the party gets sealed off."

If you were going to shut down a party and search a

mansion, the first thing you'd do is secure the exit. So that ruled out the front doors. After that, you'd alert the perimeter guards to look inward and stop people leaving. That wouldn't take long, so they couldn't just scale the walls. What did that leave them?

"Janu," Galan said. "How did you get onto the grounds?"

"Through a drain."

"You've got to be kidding," Jendora said. "I'm not going through a sewer."

"I probably wouldn't fit anyway." Grog held the bag of holding up. "And I'm not letting this go."

Why was Grog treating him like this? Galan had done nothing but try to protect his orcish friend... even if he was selling the guild out to the Sentinels.

"What's stopping me from killing you and taking the unicorn out through the catacombs?" Jendora held one of her hooked ropes by her side.

"You know what, Grog?" Galan crossed his arms. "I think that's a good idea. Hand the bag to Jendora. We'll head down to the catacombs."

"We will?" Jendora stepped back from Grog. "What about Lady Vars?"

"I thought you said it was flooded?" Janu asked.

"Forget about her," Galan said to Jendora. "With Lady Heatherdown's money we can buy anonymity." It would be safer to use the money to leave the Three Kingdoms, maybe return to Palaencia. Convincing Grog to do that wasn't going to be easy.

Grog rose to his full height, his knuckles turned white on the bag. "Why the fuck would I do that, little man? I've got everything I need right here."

"Because I know you betrayed us to the Sentinels." Galan

looked at the dirt under his nails.

"I *knew* it was you." Jendora raised the hook.

"Give up the unicorn." Galan didn't want Grog to get hurt, but his friend didn't leave him with many options. There was no way they'd make it through the catacombs and the caves without bloodshed if people didn't know their place. A pack of thieves was only strong so long as a pecking order was well established. Grog *knew* that, what was he doing?

Deep rumbles of laughter rose from Grog as he threw his head back. "So you can free the unicorn and get paid by Lady Heatherdown here? She's a druid you idiot," Grog spat. "She doesn't have any money. I'm keeping the unicorn."

"What?" Galan searched for a hint of a lie on his friend's face, but could find none.

Heatherdown took a step backwards, further down the passageway. Her eyes danced from Galan to Jendora, then to Grog. How had he missed this? He really should have paid more attention to her. Whoever heard of a druid with money?

"Then we go out the sewer," Galan said. "Or I will, with Janu. Lady Vars will buy the unicorn, but we need to meet her in the east of Kalindar valley within two days. If we go out via the catacombs we will run out of time."

"I'm not going out the sewer," Jendora warned.

"I know." Galan held his hands out to calm everyone down. "You and Grog go out the catacombs. We'll take the unicorn through the sewer and get paid. We can all meet up in Threerun later."

"I don't trust you," Jendora said. "I want my money."

"I'm not giving up the unicorn," Grog said again.

"Damn it, Grog!" Galan threw his hands up in the air.

"I've been trying to help you. I've never betrayed you. Why won't you just give me the unicorn? We can go to Palaencia, live free of all this. I can get you so much money that your family will never need to worry again."

Grog took the realisation that his secret family wasn't that secret in his stride. "Because I'm handling things on my own now, Galan. I'm going to become a druid."

"A druid!?" Galan couldn't help the mirth in his voice.

"Yes, and freeing this unicorn is my ticket in."

"You've got to be kidding!" Janu laughed. "You're a thief."

A breeze ruffled Galan's hair and flickered the lantern flames. Wait. The lanterns were covered, how was it — the lights went out. Complete darkness pressed in on them, it felt almost palpable. This wasn't just a lack of ligh—

"You're all thieves." A man's voice came from all directions, from the inky black itself.

Galan strained his eyes but couldn't see anything, not even his own hand touching his face. How close was Grog? Which direction was the wall?

Scuffing sounds passed by his head, disturbing his hair. Everyone moved at once, grabbing and shoving. A woman screamed. Grog grunted. Galan backed away and felt the wall behind him.

A flame ignited on the tip of Janu's finger. She opened one of the lanterns and lit it, pushing back the dark. The black peeled away from them, as though the light caused it pain, then faded away. Everyone checked the surroundings.

"What the fuck was that?" Janu asked.

"Where's Lady Heatherdown?" Grog asked.

Doors and lanterns flickered past as Heather flew backwards through the servant's passages. Count Radu — she *knew* he was a vampire — held onto the back of her, reeling her through the innermost parts of his mansion. Arches of rock, then stairs and ladders streamed past. He was taking her up. She remembered the many towers that dotted the mansion's skyline, they could be climbing any one of them.

She rolled along the ground on her shoulders and elbows, clouds of dust puffing up with each impact. The wall cracked as she struck it. It took a moment for her vision to clear, and a moment more for the air to settle.

They were surrounded by wood, the topmost part of a spire. But not one from his mansion, no, this was one of the palace spires, she was sure of it. Under her hands she felt stone beneath the thick layer of dust. A pigeon cooed expletives from a nest in the corner, the sanctity and serenity of its roost having been disturbed.

From the pointed ceiling, a black shape descended and unfurled itself. Count Radu touched down silently, leaning forward with his arms out wide. Incisors rested over his lower lip. Black hair hung lank across his face. Both of his eyes were intact.

He hissed. "How dare you enter my domain and threaten me."

Bones hurt and muscles complained as she pushed herself up. "Fuck off. Stop being so dramatic. Just bite me."

He flared himself back, rising as he did so and landing a few metres away. "I have no taste for Elven blood. It is foul, far too sweet. Why have you come to my dread abode?"

"I don't want you to... feed on me. Turn me into a vampire."

His arm dragged a black cape through the air. He twirled with it, covering himself in darkness and reappearing to her left. "You know not what you ask of me! Fool!"

Heather tried to grab him. "Stop fucking around. Your parlour tricks don't scare me."

"You mortals are all the same." Radu was sitting in the rafters now. "Immortality is not a curse that I can bestow upon anyone."

"*Bestow* it upon me." Maybe intimidation wasn't the best way to go about this. He was a vampire after all, fear was his game. "Please."

His cloak flapped as he drifted down again. "Tell me mortal, why do you want immortality so?"

"What do you care?'

"I have roamed this world for one hundred and eleven years. Everyone I have ever loved has died. I am alone, and nothing can satiate my sorrow. Immortality is a curse."

"I'm one hundred and twenty-five," Heather said. "And until a week ago I hadn't spoken to anyone in fifty-six years."

Radu's brow creased. He leaned forward and sniffed the air. "Ahh… you are a druid." He hissed, displaying his teeth. "You are not here to kill me?"

"I can if you want," she said. "Alleviate your pain."

"No! This curse is beyond death." More spinning and cloak whipping. "When I leave this material plane, I will be locked in the domain of Nearuul, forever tormented by the dark god."

"Fine. Then just turn me. And give me some of your money so I can buy my own mansion in another city."

"Fool! I may be a creature of the night, but I still have a conscience. I did not turn my wife and child, even when they lay dying in my arms. I will not turn another."

This was going nowhere. Heather moved to the edge of the space and found a missing tile to gaze down onto the city. Bonfires and torches could be seen nearby, pinpointing

Radu's mansion. Directly below was a paved courtyard, lit with lanterns. The catacombs must spread under many of the central buildings of Kalindar.

What was she supposed to do now? She couldn't even return to her grove, nature had abandoned her. Unless she did something to pay it back, like free a unicorn, or kill a vampire, it would never speak to her again. Never bother her with tedious requests...

...She was free. This was it. She no longer wielded the wild magic. Nature would no longer demand her attention or obedience. The druidic council might be upset, as would her parents, but none of them would do much about it. Sure, she didn't have the wealth and luxury of someone like Radu... but at least she didn't need to sleep outdoors anymore.

"I... I think I'll be going now," Heather said.

"You are a druid, yes?"

"I don't know. Kind of."

"I have a request."

Knowing now that he wasn't likely to turn anyone else into a vampire, Heather reasoned that he wasn't all that bad. There *were* natural creatures, like Legs, that did far worse than Radu did to their victims. Like those weird wasps that laid eggs in snails.

"If I can help, sure." Heather smiled.

"Cure me."

"Cure you?"

"There is only one way to rid me of this vampirism, but I cannot bring myself to do it. I am too fond of him."

"Fond of who?"

"Sunshine Sapphire Rose. I must remove his horn and ingest it if I am to rest in peace."

"You need to eat the unicorn to die?"

"Just his horn," Radu clarified.

"Removing his horn will kill him?"

"Yes. I cannot. Killing such a wonderful creature is beyond even my dark cruelty."

"But you'll eat the horn if I kill him for you?"

"Yes. Like a child who doesn't want to consider where meat comes from."

Killing the unicorn to remove a vampire from the world... Those two things would even each other out, wouldn't they? She'd still be on nature's bad side, still safe from its endless needs.

"Why should I help you?" Heather asked.

"Because if you don't, I will kill you. And if you do, I will leave my estate to you."

This is exactly what she'd set out to do, jump free of the shackles of druidic duties and land in the soft lap of civilised opulence.

"Okay," Heather said. "Let's go slaughter a unicorn."

CHAPTER THIRTEEN

Now What?

JANU STOOD WITH her back against the wall, unsure what to do. The thieves had the unicorn, but there were too many to arrest by herself. Would Marrid and Ainsworth hold off from attacking her on sight? She hadn't heard them commanding Gwyn to stop tossing fireballs. Plus the vampire was upset now and could be back at any moment.

"We need to go look for Heatherdown." Grog started up a corridor.

Galan grabbed at his arm. "No we don't. That's a fucking vampire and she hasn't got any money."

"I need her to tell me where to find the druid council." Grog pulled himself free and continued on.

"You can't be serious about this," Galan called out. "Think about your family."

"I *am.*"

The only one Janu really wanted was Galan, but she needed to get him separated from the others, with the unicorn. "Grog's right," Janu interjected. "He needs to find your druid friend."

"No he *doesn't*," Galan said.

"And what about the unicorn?" Jendora cracked a hook against a panel of wood behind her, hard. "You're not taking that unicorn with you."

"Hold on." Janu softened her voice. "Please. Just listen, all of you. I have a plan."

"Great, a fucking plan." Galan rolled his eyes. "You Sentinels couldn't come up with a plan to get lunch."

"Just shut up," Grog boomed. "What is it?"

Janu took a deep breath, more to give everyone else a moment of calm than for herself. "There are Sentinels looking for us. If we're going to get that unicorn out, we're going to have to sneak it out. The best way to sneak it out is through the sewer. Only Galan and I can fit through there."

"Fuck off," Jendora shoved Janu against the wall. "We take it through the catacombs."

"You can't." Janu closed her eyes. There had to be a good reason. "You can't because they know about it. They're going to be waiting for you there."

"*Shit.*" Grog stomped. The walls shook.

Janu waved some of the falling dust away. "And you won't get it out through the front doors, not now."

"Wait! The front doors. Yes we can!" Galan said. "Elvalor. The guards don't know about him. He's still out there singing. For all they know, he's just an entertainer, he can walk out with it."

"What the fuck?" Grog held the bag of holding away from his body.

It moved. Hoof prints pushed out against the fabric from the inside. He opened the top, peered in, and reeled back. The sudden emergence of Sapphire Sunshine Rose's head caused him to drop the bag and stumble backwards.

"Ouch," Sunshine Sapphire Rose said. "Watch it."

Just the head was poking out of the bag, laying on its side on the floor.

"It's really dark in there," Sunshine Sapphire Rose said. "And I think I was running out of air."

"Sorry," Grog said. "I forgot."

"Where's the molasses?" Sunshine Sapphire Rose asked. "I was told that there would be molasses and yet here we all are, sans molasses."

"It will be a little while," Janu said. "We're just trying to figure out the best way to go about it."

"We've decided on it," Galan declared. "Elvalor can sneak it out, the rest of us can go out via sewers or caves, whatever they want, and meet up later."

Damn it. There had to be another way to separate Galan and the unicorn from the rest of them.

"Why are we sneaking out molasses?" Sunshine Sapphire Rose looked as confused as a unicorn could.

Grog picked the bag up and shoved the unicorn head back inside.

"Hold on!" The unicorn's cries were muffled around Grog's hand.

With a final shove, the bag was sealed again.

"Here." Grog held the unicorn bag out to Galan. "If I can't let it free, it's not much use to me. Go and sell it, make some money."

Galan took the bag and gazed up at Grog. Their hands lingered. What was with these two?

"Mate... I'm sorry. If I knew you wanted to be a druid, I would have helped you steal it from the get go."

"Fuck *off*." Jendora raised a hook. "We're selling that

stupid fucking thing. Let's go find Elvalor and tell him the score."

"Fine, I'm going to go find Lady Heatherdown," Grog said.

"Mate... why?" Galan asked.

"Because I made a deal. I'm not going to back out of it now. Maybe she can still get me in as a druid..."

"Alright, let's go then." Galan stepped up to Grog's side.

Grog raised an eyebrow at Galan. "What are you doing?"

"Coming with you. This whole fucking circus was to help you and your family. I just wanted to make sure you went on your way with a good pay-day." He held the bag out to Jendora without taking his eyes off Grog.

"No, get the unicorn out," Grog said. "At least if I can't be a druid, I can have a bit of coin."

The two of them continued to gaze at each other like idiots. Without another word, Galan patted Grog on the back as the half-orc left.

With a clap of his hands, Galan leapt to the start of a different passageway. "Right. Let's go."

All attempts at stealth seemed to be done away with now. Every door they came across was yanked open and investigated. Bed-chambers, hallways, ballrooms, it didn't matter. If it wasn't a garden or the kitchen, they raced on. It seemed cavalier to Janu, but Galan *was* a professional.

A clank in the darkness behind them drew nervous looks. The vampire. How could they forget so quickly? Galan stared into the dark over Janu's shoulder.

"Do you think he'll be alright?" Galan asked her.

"Of course." She had to allay his fears, she couldn't risk him running off now. "He's a big guy, Radu would be no match for him."

He pulled his eyes away and kept on.

Eventually they came across a ladder that lowered them down into a pantry, with an open door into a kitchen. Chefs and waiters rushed about, plating meals and rolling things into pastry. Every scent reminded Janu that it had been a long time since she last ate.

"This is the one," Galan said. "Elvalor is out there playing now."

With the same air of authority that Janu used to walk down a busy road in Threerun, Galan walked across the kitchen. She did the same. Openly shocked faces watched them. Conversation died down.

"This isn't going to work," Jendora whispered.

"Yes it will," Galan said. "Act like you're doing nothing wrong and no one will ask questions."

They crossed the kitchen without being challenged and entered a hall full of party guests. These people parted much slower, gawking and talking about them openly. Galan smiled, did a little jog to the left or right as they made their way toward the garden. Did he think that would work, making them look like entertainment? She was covered in shit!

Elvalor's song ended the moment he spied them in the crowd. He too smiled and waved at the guests as he hopped off the stage and strode up to them. Though focused on Galan, he gave Janu a slight nod of acknowledgement.

"Where the fuck have you been?" he said to Galan. "I was about to think you all fucked off without me."

Galan pulled him down to his level and wrapped an arm around the elf's shoulders. "It's time to go."

"They got it? They're clear down to the caves?"

"No." Galan held the bag in front of them as they walked.

"You need to get it out of here."

This was Janu's last chance. She needed to say something, do anything to stop that unicorn leaving Galan's possession. *And* find some way to get him alone to be arrested.

"I think the sewer would be better," Janu said. "Galan, can we trust this guy to take the unicorn?"

"Keep your voice down." Elvalor leaned back, slapped Galan on the back, and pretended to laugh.

They both pointed like the joke was at the expense of the other.

"If they're waiting in the catacombs, it means that they're locking the place down tight," Galan said as he laughed. "They might be checking the drains as well. Best way out is in the open now."

A blinding light elicited cries of astonishment from the guests. It came from above them, in a brilliant flash of iridescence that took a few seconds to fade away. In its place, Gwyn Ainsworth floated in the air.

"The party is over!" she called out over the garden. "Count Radu asks that you all leave the premises immediately. Oh, except you four." Her finger pointed to them. "I want that unicorn."

THIS UNICORN WAS really starting to seem like too much trouble for what it was worth. Well no, actually. It was worth more money than Galan had ever had in his life. He could buy a city, or even a kingdom with that kind of money. Grog and his family would never know the feeling of a cold night in an alley, or having to sit with your back against the wall in every tavern.

"Drop the unicorn bag," the spell-wielding woman sang

out.

"Not bloody likely," Galan muttered.

All pretentiousness evaporated as soon as the first fireball hit. Party guests scattered in chaos, shoving past acquaintances, knocking tables over. All the deference shown by the servants was snatched away by the stampede toward the doors of the mansion. Glass broke. People screamed.

Another fireball lit up the scene.

"Fuck! Run!" Jendora shouted.

An elderly gentleman careened toward them, arms outstretched, glancing over his shoulder at the flames licking the night. Jendora spun and shouldered him into a nearby group of party goers, crashing them all into a heap.

That was all the impetus Galan needed to start moving. With the bag clutched in his hands, he ran toward the mansion. Elvalor, Janu, and Jendora ran with him, shoving and shouting people out of the way. The lower panels of glass on the left-most door were gone, uneven edges of timber hung down from above.

The hall was full. People crammed and climbed toward the few narrow exits. Even the hidden doors sat wide open, with both guests and waiters scrambling to get through.

Glass and ash rained down.

"I want that unicor—" The magic woman's words were replaced with a scream of fear and pain.

Legs was on her back, wrapped around her torso and head. It struck the back of her neck and fell with her onto the grass outside the doors, hidden behind a wall of wailing people.

Lady Heatherdown emerged from the crowd beside Galan, her hand reaching out to him. "Give me the unicorn, quickly."

"No, she— she's in the thrall of Radu!" Janu slapped Heatherdown's hands away.

"What?" Galan couldn't see the magic woman rising. Grog barely survived a bite from Legs, was the magic woman dead?

"I must have the unicorn," Heatherdown said. "A million coins of whatever metal you want."

A million? Did she think he was an idiot? There wasn't that much money in the kingdom, and Grog had already confessed that the druid was broke. Could vampires control people?

"Not a chance," Galan said.

Elvalor kicked the druid into a group of fleeing guests. "Run!"

As they pushed deeper into the rush of people, Janu stepped to the front and tried to clear a path. Her shouted orders went unheard, or more realistically, ignored. Fists and feet did little to make a dent in the crush of people. Someone even punched back.

"It's no use." Janu nursed her jaw. "There has to be another way."

"Over there." Elvalor threw something at a window, breaking it.

Galan sprinted, clutched the bag against his chest, and jumped. His feet gave out as he hit cobblestone, rolling him across the ground. The side of a parked cart stopped his legs, his head cracked against a mounting block. Blurriness pushed against the edges of his vision.

Unsure guards stood around them as Elvalor and Jendora pulled him to his feet. People ran in all directions. Shouted orders from further along the road called for buckets and a chain-gang.

"We should split up," Janu said. "Flee the city and meet up back in Threerun."

Galan's head hurt, his thoughts felt cloudy, unformed, nebulous. Why would they split up? Heatherdown had asked for the unicorn, but she didn't have any money, was she trying to swindle him?

"Wait," Galan said. "Just give me a minute to catch my wits..."

"There's no time," Janu shouted. "The Sentinels will be on us soon. If we split up, they won't know who to go after."

That seemed reasonable.

Janu pointed at Elvalor and Jendora. "You two, go that way. We'll go this way." She pulled Galan along with her.

"No fucking way." Jendora grabbed Galan's arm. "I'm not leaving that unicorn with you."

"We don't have time for this," Janu said. "There's only one gate to the city, and down that way is faster. You'll get there first. We won't be able to get past you."

Elvalor and Jendora looked at each other.

"Can you even complete the sale with the buyer?" Janu asked. "Will they trade with you or is it a deal Galan made?"

What was Janu talking about? Anyone could make the sale... did she not trust the others? What did she know that he didn't?

Jendora and Elvalor ran off, parallel to the mansion, while Galan and Janu ran directly away from it. Guests were starting to get out past the guards and rush around the carriages. Behind them, red flickers glowed from within some of the windows. A flame flickered from one and touched the eave above. People launched themselves from others nearby.

Galan's head was starting to clear. "Where are we

going?"

"We need to get away from all this chaos. I don't know if Gwyn is following us."

"Who?"

"Gwyn Ainsworth." She looked at him expectantly. "The fireballs. That woman."

"How do you know her? Is she a Sentinel?"

"No. Yes. I'm not sure. But it isn't safe here." She pushed him forward a little. "Do you still have the unicorn?"

"Yeah, it's here." He patted the bag.

"We need to find somewhere to lay low."

"No." Why would they hang around waiting to be found? "It would be better to make a run for it now, while everyone else is fleeing. We only need to get as far as Lady Vars in the east."

"Trust me," Janu said. "It would be better for us to hide for now."

Trust her? What possible reason did he have to trust her? She might be corrupt, but that was a reason to *not* trust her. You didn't lead the Thieves' Guild for as long as he had without knowing *that*. But she did ensure that the unicorn wasn't handed over to Elvalor and Jendora... he trusted them even less. What was her angle? Did *she* want the unicorn?

Something clicked into place. How would she know the Sentinels were waiting in the catacombs? The first she'd heard about his planned exit was when they told her the caves were flooded. How could he have misjudged so badly *again*? She wasn't corrupt. She was manipulating him, waiting to get him alone.

"Alright," he said. "Let's hide down one of these alleyways until we know what's going on."

* * *

SOMEONE STEPPED ON Heather's arm. Then someone else stepped on her foot.

"Fuck!" She tried to get up, but was trapped under a portly woman. "Get off me!"

Heather shoved the woman and extricated herself. A fire burned against the side of the mansion, flames climbed up the edges of the massive length of bunched fabric next to the doors. People were confused and panicked. Where did Galan go with the unicorn?

Spidery thoughts slipped into the back of her mind. Legs had subdued the woman that attacked them, she was probably dead. Strange that Heather's bond with Legs wasn't severed along with her other powers. Her teachers had always told her that the animal companion was a gift of nature. But now she wasn't sure what it was.

The crowd was thinning out. Where was she? The mansion was ahead of her, catching on fire, at least the trappings that weren't made of stone. The garden she was in was walled on all sides. They could have only gone inside.

"Heatherdown!"

A meaty arm waved at her from inside the mansion. It was Grog, no one else could have towered over the crowd as he did. She jogged up to the doors and dived under the flames. In a frenzy, someone bumped into Grog, it didn't budge him in the slightest.

"What happened?" he asked her. "Where did Radu take you?"

"We spoke is all. Where is Galan? Where is the unicorn?"

"I don't know."

"I need it." There was too many ways out from here, Galan could have gone anywhere.

"To free it?"

"No. Fuck the unicorn. To kill it."

He took a step back, the fire by the windows reflected sharply in his eyes. "What for? It didn't harm you."

Her lessons on the ferocity of orc-kind burst to the front of her mind. "Yeah, it didn't. But a unicorn horn can cleanse Radu of vampirism, thereby harming less people overall." That seemed like a reasonable justification if questioned by the council.

"Huh." He put one hand on his hip, the other scratched above his brow. "So, nature cares more about long-term sustainability than short term gains... and that would look good to the council?"

The few remaining people scampered out of the hall, leaving nothing but trampled food and tables.

"Something like that," she confirmed.

"Well... Galan *had* the unicorn. He was going to give it Elvalor to sneak it out of here."

"I don't think so," she said. "They were all running away with it together."

Grog looked around at the fire slowly encroaching on their safety. "What happened here? That fireball lady?"

"Yeah, but she should be dead now." Heather glanced back. "Spider bite."

A man's voice rang out. "Dead?! What have you done with my mother?"

The man was tall, dressed in thick leather armour, and looked very strong. Grog stood taller and looked stronger, but wore no armour. As the man drew a sword, Heather caught sight of the yellow Sentinel rose stitched across his breast. He came from one of the mansion's hallways.

"Ainsworth, don't act too rash," another voice said from

behind them. "An orc, even unarmed, isn't to be trifled with."

It was a dwarf, the same that she saw in the cave and in the window she was blasted out of. Metal armour, marked by soot in a few places, covered him from chest to toe. He held a war-axe at the ready, his expression was hard. Where he came from, Heather couldn't guess... had he snuck up on them?

"Shut up, Marrid! You're both under arrest," Ainsworth said. "For the attempted murder of Count Radu of Kalindar, of conspiracy to commit grand theft... rustling, starting a fire —"

"—we didn't start the fire," Heather said. "That dead woman over there did. She threw fireballs at those lovely fabric things next to the windows."

Ainsworth kept his sword tip pointed at them as he walked around to the doors. The dwarf, Marrid, moved like the opposite side of the needle, keeping her and Grog skewered between them. Grog yawned.

When Ainsworth was outside, he backed down the two stairs and glanced at the grass. He stifled a sound from his throat. "And you're under arrest for murder."

"We didn't kill her," Grog said. "A giant spider did."

"Check her body," Heather added. "You'll find four to eight puncture wounds, spaced a few inches apart."

His sword fell flat on the ground as he dropped to a knee and pulled the back of the dead woman's dress aside. Heather didn't need a connection to the natural world to know he was holding back tears. A single sob erupted before he cut it off, rising red-faced, with white knuckles on his sword hilt. His voice came thick. "No. You commanded the spider," he said. "I heard the reports."

"Whoever heard of commanding a spider to do

anything," Grog said. "You give us way too much credit. We're simple thieves."

"You are. But she isn't." Ainsworth sniffed, set his jaw, and lowered his gaze. "She's a druid."

"No I'm not a druid," Heather said. She didn't add how recent her negative-druid status was.

"It doesn't matter." Marrid spoke to Ainsworth rather than Heather or Grog. "We arrest them and bring them in for interrogation."

"I haven't got time for this," Heather declared. "I've got to stop Galan from getting away with the unicorn."

"What?" the dwarf said.

"Galan is getting away with the unicorn, Radu asked me to stop him."

"I don't care," Ainsworth declared. "You're under arrest. Put your hands behind your back, and get to your knees."

"No." Grog folded his arms.

"You're under arrest," Ainsworth's voice broke into a screech. "Obey!"

Grog smirked. "Or what?"

No animal in the wild would dream of provoking another. Well... maybe cubs and kittens, things that made games of pretend adventure, but Grog was no baby orc. Why then, did he wilfully bring on the assault?

Ainsworth lost what little control he had left and surged forward, bounding up the two stairs, his blade set for an overhead swing. Grog remained as he was until the last second, stepped to the side, and rammed his fist up into the man's stomach. Despite the leather armour, bone cracked. If there was any air left in Ainsworth's lungs, he would have screamed, but instead gave only a ragged intake of air.

He collapsed over Grog's fist and was cast to the side,

rolling and clutching his body. Once again his sword lay forgotten. Grog retrieved and inspected it in the firelight.

"Do you really want to do this?" he asked Marrid.

"Not particularly, no." Marrid set his feet apart. "But I will."

"You're not even a Sentinel," Grog said. "You haven't got the stupid yellow rose on your chest."

Marrid spat. "What do you know of the Sentinels?"

"I know that you followed us here by watching for my crosses."

A groan escaped Ainsworth on the ground. "*You're* the informant?"

"Yes." Grog ran a finger down the length of the sword.

"Did you kill that woman?" Marrid stepped sideways, toward Ainsworth.

"No," Grog said.

"We told you, it was a giant spider," Heather added.

Married narrowed his eyes. "You're not in command of the spider?"

Grog laughed, then nudged Heather. She laughed too.

Marrid lowered his guard and removed a hand from the axe. Grog shifted slightly forward, like he was going to make a move, but changed his mind. Ainsworth was helped to his feet.

"Can you walk?" Marrid asked him.

"No."

"I don't know what's going on," Marrid said to Grog and Heather. "But I've got no hope of stopping both of you. If you're as you say, an informant, on our side, go. Find Galan and stop him. We'll make sure you get paid."

Grog nodded, grabbed Heather's shoulder, and urged her through a door and into a hallway.

"Where are we going?" she asked him.

"We're looking for a way out, we gotta find Galan, get that unicorn, and cure Radu."

"So, you're on board?" she asked.

"Yes. But you need to introduce me to the druid council. Get me in. Galan will still want to get paid, so the druid council will have to make amends."

There was a distinct possibility that the druidic council would not see things the way that Heather did. A vampire was a horribly unnatural thing to leave alive, curing it might be seen as a reverse-desecration. But a unicorn was a near-extinct creature, bordering on mythical. Its death would not be appreciated, even if in the service of vampire removal.

Heather studied the burning and charred trappings of wealth. Even though it was destroyed, it was better than the grove. "They've got the money they set aside to pay for the theft. Deal."

CHAPTER FOURTEEN

Arrest

THE ALLEY WAS narrow, barely wide enough for a gnome and a halfling, let alone the mostly human-sized denizens of Kalindar. Above them, the eaves overlapped and jutted against each other, ensuring that even at high noon it would be dark. Now, with an overcast sky in the middle of the night, it was... well Janu couldn't see a damned thing.

"Just a little bit further in," Galan said. "Best if we're not seen."

Janu caught her foot on something. A barrel or a pipe maybe. As soon as her eyes adjusted she would make the arrest. Maybe wait until his back was turned and then jump on him. She'd need to be sure to grab the bag too, if the unicorn fell out in here, well, it would either break through the stone walls on either side or be broken by them.

"Down here, Janu." Galan sounded further along than she realised he was. "We should be alright down here."

A wall appeared in front of her just before she walked into it. It felt slick from the recent rain. With the lack of any cleansing daylight it was probably covered in grime and sludge. She wiped her hand on her pants but then remembered how filthy they were. There was nowhere else to wipe them.

"I think we're far enough." Janu peered ahead. A wall there, a sliver of starlight above. Was that a barrel? No, it was Galan. "Let's…. Um. Have a little break and work out what to do next."

"Yes," Galan said. "Let's."

He stood there. Watching her.

"So," she said. "Do you think we need to worry about Radu coming after us?"

"I'm a little more worried about you." A glimmer of steel sparkled where his hands would be.

"Stop it, Galan. It's over. You're under arrest for grand theft of a magical creature."

"Is that even a crime?" Why did he sound like he'd moved, he was still right there… wasn't he?

"Yes." She reached for her sword. Shit! She didn't have one. All those knives he carried… how many more could he possibly have? "This will be easier for both of us if you come willingly."

"It would be easier if you gave up the act and help me sell this unicorn."

"I can't do that."

"Why?" He honestly sounded incredulous. "I've heard about where you came from. You know what it's like in these dark alleys."

How dare he bring her past into this. They weren't the same. She only ever stole to survive. He stole to cushion his life. "There are two different kinds of people in the gutter, Galan."

"Is that right?"

"Yeah. It is. There's those who had no chance. They were put there, and they struggle, and sometimes they claw themselves out and they wash away the shit. And there's people like you who prey on them."

"And which kind are you? I'm still in the gutter. Haven't got a coin to my name, trying to survive and pull myself, and Grog, out of this life. And here you are, arresting me to bolster your position in the Sentinels."

"Fuck you. You'd steal the bread from an orphan's hand if you were peckish."

"Only because I put the fucking bread in those hands and I would again later that night."

"What are you talking about?"

"You ever notice how all those little urchins weren't dying in your gutters anymore? Ever notice how those old rich fucks had started shipping their servants in from Southport? Huh? Notice that those pick-pockets in the market all had shoes? Who do you think did that?"

She had noticed. Every time she walked the streets she noticed. That was where she came from, that was her life not so long ago. The Sentinels acted for those people. At least, Janu always strived for that. How the orphans fared was how she measured the success of the Sentinels.

"Yeah I noticed. Lowering crime-rates will do that."

Galan laughed. "You think that was you? Do you think locking down the slums and combing through it with overzealous city-guards did anything for the people that lived down there? Have you forgotten what it's like? Every one of those criminals was someone trying to feed their family.

"No, all you did was stop what little control there was

over it. The thieves' guild clothed those children, taught them skills to live by. Skills you would've learned yourself once upon a time."

If true, that would mean that she'd done to people what she'd joined the Sentinels to stop. "No. I cleaned the streets."

"The problem wasn't in the streets, and you know it."

He was right. She did know it. People were born into their positions. Even her. Sure, she'd scrambled out of the gutter and made something of herself. And where was she now? In a dark alley, consorting with the underbelly of the city. It didn't matter how you struggled against the constraints, you did what you were made for.

Janu stamped a foot. "We arrest anyone who commits crime."

"Some crimes are of necessity, Janu. You stole for food."

"My past has nothing to do with this."

"It has everything to do with it." Galan stepped into a thin slice of grey light. "You're trying to stop what happened to you from happening again. But you can't. I can't either. The best we can do is help when it does happen. That's why Grog and I started the thieves' guild."

"No it isn't, you two wanted to get rich."

"Yes, that too. And we brought a lot of people up with us. You want to help the orphan's don't you? The folk who never had a choice?"

"Yes."

"Well, what do you care if I steal from some merchant with more money than sense? Shit, you should help me if you really want to make a difference."

"I arrest the merchants for crimes too!"

"Except most of what they do isn't a crime, even if it hurts everyone below them. What happens if they don't pay a kid the wages they worked for? That kid can't afford to take it to the court. He hasn't got any money."

She stood in silence for a while. There were a hundred situations like what Galan was describing where the wealthy could get away with it. And in all of them, there was nothing she could do to stop it. Not as a Sentinel, not even as a criminal. But maybe if she was both. "Okay," she said. "What now?"

"Same as we were doing before. We work together. I help you to make arrests, the people on the street who are taking more than they should, who step on too many people. In turn, you let us operate and help those we can."

"I thought you were getting out of it. You and Grog."

"Looks like Grog has figured out his own path. I don't think he needs me anymore. This is what I was made to do."

"Where is Lady Vars?"

"Outside the city, on the other side of the valley, a few hours walk at most."

"Let's get going then," Janu said. "The sooner this is done, the sooner we can get back to Threerun."

Galan condensed from the darkness next to where Janu thought he was. A knife disappeared behind his hand. After they emerged into the street, Galan looked both ways and bent down, opening the unicorn bag as he did.

"Let's check the merchandise," he said. "Come on Sunshine Sapphire Rose."

No muzzle emerged. No horn.

"Hey, come on."

When still nothing came forth, he creased his brow and reached in.

"Gimme a hand," he said.

Janu knelt beside him and felt inside the bag. Her hands

brushed something coarse, hair, and skin. She reached around the thing and pulled. The head of the unicorn emerged from the bag, its tongue lolling out the side of its mouth, the white of its eyes showing.

"Fuck," Galan said. "It's dead."

LIKE A PROVOKED ant nest, the people of Kalindar rushed about in every direction. No one seemed sure of what was happening, only that there was danger, that action needed to be taken. Plain-clothed workers dragged their nervous families away from home, guards ran past Heather in twos, searching for whoever they were supposed to fight.

People passed on warnings of giant spiders, vampires, lunatic wizards, and roaming hordes of barbaric orcs attacking at will. Every alley and road was dangerous, there was nowhere to hide. Fire spread. The city was evacuating and hunkering down at the same time.

"Where would they go?" Heather asked Grog. "To get the unicorn out?"

"There's only one way out that I know of," Grog said. "The front gates."

Heather remembered their approach to the city, and the absolute barrier that the city's walls created. The gates were the obvious choice.

"Let's go."

The crowds thickened as Heather and Grog got sight of the city exit. A fully laden wagon sat in the centre of the road with a broken axle, a red faced merchant standing atop it, directing orders to a gang of city-guards. People shoved around the guards and wagon to escape the city, upsetting the merchant's attempts to both protect his wares and right his vehicle.

Enterprising commoners grabbed what they could as they passed, emboldening others to follow suit. As Heather and Grog approached, a portly man climbed the back of a patiently waiting cart and took off with a small crate.

"The looting is starting," Grog said. "Must be the fire, tends to get people worked up."

"What's 'looting'?" Heather asked.

"It's when everything gets very dangerous."

"What about the unicorn, where would Galan be?"

"He must be on foot," Grog said. "You can track him from the other side of the gate."

"I hope so," Heather said to herself.

Standing near Grog made progress through the crush of people less onerous than it would have been. All he had to do was clear his throat or politely excuse himself and people pressed themselves against the wall and did whatever they could to make his way easier. Shadowy figures filled the area outside the city, standing aimlessly in little clumps. The road south bristled with what few figures could be seen in the scant moonlight.

"Heather, Grog." Elvalor emerged from the throng. "We've been waiting for Galan and Janu. Have you seen them?"

"No." Grog gazed at the red glow emanating from deep within the walled city. "Do they have the unicorn?"

"Yes," Jendora confirmed.

Heather checked the face of every child-sized person that rushed past the wagon-blocked gate, but saw no sign of Galan or Janu. With the way the city was built, wall to wall and roof to roof, the mansion's fire was spreading. Judging by the coughs and blackened faces that were starting to appear, the whole city could burn.

"Should we go in after them?" Grog asked.

"There's no need." Jendora pointed up the wall.

From a tall guard tower next to the gate, Galan and Janu stepped out onto a narrow ledge of stone beneath a window. A rope was already hanging down. Their hesitation was clear.

Heather felt down into the stony soil and pleaded with nature to help. A gnarled and knotted vine was all that was needed, something to provide good footholds for their descent. It would only take a moment to grow and if nature wanted her to rid the world of a vampire, it needed to help.

Nothing.

"Come on!" Jendora ran toward the wall, unwinding a rope from her belt. She tossed the hooked end over the wall, pulled it taught, and then took it across Janu and Galan's path. It wasn't much, but at least there was one more rope for them to use.

"What can I do?" Heather asked.

No one answered as Galan and Janu swung themselves over the lip and descended the rope. Both of them had wrapped it around their torsos and stood horizontally against the tower, feeding the loop and walking backwards. It was slow, but safe. Heather held her breath.

When they reached the ground, Elvalor rushed forward and snatched the bag from Galan, who made no attempt to prevent it being taken. In turn, Jendora tore it from Elvalor's grip, backed away and opened it. She gasped and let it fall. Sunshine Sapphire Rose fell partially out and flopped to the side, a lifeless hoof in the air.

"It's dead?" Jendora nudged it with her foot.

"Yeah," Galan said. "Suffocated, I think."

"That makes things easier," Grog said to Heather. "I was

worried about how we were going to do that."

Heather had to admit, she wasn't looking forward to that part.

"Do what?" Janu asked.

"Kill it," Heather announced. "We need the horn to cure Radu."

"Cure?" Elvalor asked.

Heather shrugged. "He wants to die."

"The horn still has some power?" Elvalor asked.

Before she could confirm, Jendora gripped and pulled the bag toward her, disappearing the unicorn into its folds.

Elvalor lurched backwards and thrust his lute at the others, his fingers poised over the strings. "Stay back! I know a death song! I'll use it if I have to."

"What are you doing?" Galan didn't seem surprised or worried.

"Jendora and I have come to an agreement. Let us go and we'll give you twenty percent of whatever we sell it for. You can divvy that up amongst yourselves."

"No." Grog folded his arms and lifted his chin. "I need to kill the vampire to become a druid."

"Yeah." Galan stepped up to Grog's side and mimicked his friend's stance. "Give him the unicorn."

"Galan, what are you doing?" Janu reached down for a sword that wasn't there. "We need it to get the guild going."

"Hold on!" Heather held her palms up. "Money! You all want some money, right?"

Everyone side-eyed each other through the tension, arms held at the ready, feet set apart.

"Radu has promised me his fortune if I kill him. I'll pay you for the unicorn, after he's dead."

Grog's brow sloped down over his eyes. "He did?"

"Yes."

"And the druid council?"

"They will be very happy that you helped destroy an undead creature of the night."

"How much?" Elvalor held the lute out and stepped into a protective position in front of Jendora.

Heather shrugged. She didn't want to give up too much of her soon-to-be wealth so fast. With the medical care she could afford, and her elven heritage, she needed it to last her for at least another six hundred years. "Twenty percent of the fortune."

"No deal," Jendora spat. "The horn on its own is still worth more than all the gold in Kalindar."

Elvalor's eyes shone out from behind the lute. "I told you Galan. It wasn't coming out of my cut."

Galan smiled, put his hands behind his back and stared at Elvalor. "If you do this, you won't be safe anywhere in the Three Kingd—"

"—I demand that unicorn!"

The young man, Ainsworth, stalked toward them, head down and smoke blackened. "My mother has been killed. The unicorn can bring her back."

"Ainsworth, stand down," Janu said. "You don't understand what's at stake." She looked around the group and lowered her voice. "Who killed his mum?"

"It was Legs," Heather admitted. "He was just trying to help."

"Jendora! Janu!" Marrid appeared behind Ainsworth. "Give yourselves up. You need to answer for your crimes and die with whatever rags of honour you can still grasp."

Without any further words, both men sprinted forward, sword and axe at the ready.

* * *

BATTLES WERE NOT where Galan shined. A battle of wits maybe. A drinking competition at a stretch. But an honest to goodness battle with blades and hammers and blood was something he made a point of avoiding. At all costs.

So when Marrid and Ainsworth charged across the stony dirt toward them, blades glinting blue moonlight and red fire, he did what he usually did when faced with charging, blade wielding enemies.

He ran.

Straight to Grog.

"We're in for it now." Galan flicked his last two knives ready.

Ainsworth struggled with the pace, one hand held across his midsection. But where he faltered, Marrid surged, making a beeline to Jendora and the bag. Elvalor stepped in front of her, his fingers dancing over the lute's strings.

It wasn't a bad song, but he didn't get much of it out before Lady Heatherdown threw a stone and cracked him in the side of the head. His body crumbled beneath the instrument, its last note ringing melancholy as it fell.

"Good shot," Galan said.

Jendora stared at Heather and stumbled backwards before suddenly flying into the sky and crashing into the dirt. A flutter of dark fabric with red trimming landed atop her prone body and seized the bag.

With a skid of stone and dirt, Marrid stopped, holding his war axe protectively in front of him. "Nosferatu!" he said.

Yellow, serpentine eyes flashed out of the fabric before it whirled and spun, leaving Radu standing tall over Jendora's body. With a flourish, the vampire upended the bag of holding.

The corpse of Sunshine Sapphire Rose collapsed onto the ground. Its eyes were open, rolled back into the head. A slack tongue lay across its horse-faced grimace.

Radu stared at it. "What have you done?"

"You can eat the horn now," Heatherdown said.

"I can help you break it off if you like." Grog walked forward. "I doubt it would be easy for a scrawny guy like—"

"—No! I had changed my mind! I'd rather live this life of endless agony than remove such a heavenly creature from this world!"

"It's a bit late for a change of heart now," Heatherdown said. "Just, eat up, and hand over the keys. Or don't hand over the keys, I'm sure I'll find them after you... expire."

"None of you deserve to live!" Radu flew at Heatherdown. Not a jump, or a leap, but flew, arms outstretched and a monstrous snarl over his face. She yelped, ducked, and frantically tried to dislodge the vampiric fingers grasping at her hair.

This seemed like as good a time as any to secure the loot, so Galan dashed over to the unicorn and tried to yank the bag of holding back over the top of it. If Grog couldn't use it to kill Radu, at least they might still be able to get something for it with Lady Vars. In the end, if his friend can't have his druid ambitions fulfilled, at least when they returned to Threerun they could live comfortably.

Janu's hand touched the bag alongside his. "What are you going to do?"

"What we agreed. Sell the unicorn, start the guild, fix Threerun."

She nodded and let the bag go.

Radu choked and spluttered against the axe shaft crushing his throat. Behind him, Marrid groaned with exertion and tried to hold on against the powerful throes of the vampire. Grog entered the fray and forced Radu down on top of Marrid, pinning them both beneath him. All three struggled with the axe.

A nearby shadow of movement formed into Heather, rolling up from the ground. She plunged her hand into the dirt and removed a tree root. Short, stout, and pointed. With a scream, she forced her way between Grog's arms and crushed the stake into Radu's chest.

Her voice shattered as she was thrown from the melee and rolled across the ground. Radu's body convulsed, paused, and with a faint smile, went limp. Grog rose and shoved the body away as clouds of dust swept up from the vampire's skin. He reached down and pulled Marrid to his feet by the axe shaft.

Grog and Marrid stepped away from each other with a polite nod. Janu stood a few steps away from Galan. Evacuees of the city stood in a loose circle surrounding them, keeping their distance and muttering quietly. Heather, Jendora, and Elvalor's bodies remained on the dirt, hopefully they were all unconscious.

"What now?" Marrid winced as he rotated a shoulder.

"Jendora is there." Janu pointed to the still unconscious body. "You can take her home to answer for her crimes. And leave the rest of this here to me. I never turned criminal."

"That's right," Galan lied. "She had me fooled though."

Marrid nodded. "And you?"

"We have the horn," Galan said. "Worth enough to get Threerun on track."

"No!" Ainsworth pointed a sword tip at the back of Galan's neck. "Give me the horn." Shit, he'd forgotten about him.

Janu turned to face Ainsworth, holding a careful hand out. "Ainsworth—"

"—my mother. Janu. She's dead. The unicorn horn can bring her back."

"Let Peter have it," Marrid said.

Janu's eyes fell on Galan. Cold steel touched the centre of his shoulders.

Grog looked on, as stoic as ever. How could Galan let the bag go now, after everything they'd been through? This was the heist to solve all his problems, to finally get his friend everything that Galan had promised him when they first started out.

A groan brought Grog's attention to Lady Heatherdown's body. He knelt down and slung her over his shoulder.

"Is she alright?" Galan asked him.

"Yeah, she'll live," he said.

"You're sure about being a druid?"

The nod from Grog was all the permission Galan needed. "Here." He handed the bag to Ainsworth. "Go."

"But just ask your mum to leave us alone," Janu added. "And I heard they need a new Captain up here, you might want to apply."

Ainsworth took the bag and hesitated. "The captain is dead. What am I supposed to tell then local council?"

Galan pointed at Elvalor laid out on the ground. "He's the man *I* saw stab the Captain." That should tie up that loose end.

The fires had grown in intensity, more people were fleeing, and coming to a stop at the strange performance outside the city gates.

Galan clapped his hands. "Come on," he said to Janu.

"We've got places to be."

The road back to Threerun would be hard without any provisions, but judging by the number of fleeing merchants, they'd manage to get home with a bit of thievery.

CHAPTER FIFTEEN

End

HEATHER AWOKE WITH her back against a twisted, miserable apple tree. Its seed had fallen in a forest some distance away and was carried here by a bird who copped a hunter's arrow through a wing. The little pod of life had skittered across the rocks of the hillside and landed in a sandy fissure. Rain eventually came and forced a sapling to emerge.

Life had been nothing but struggle for the apple tree, and it hadn't had anyone to complain to since it sprouted.

Enough, Heather told it. *No one cares. Just grow, drop apples, and do what you're supposed to.*

Appropriately chastised, the tree dropped a shrivelled, sour fruit on her head.

Where was she? Last she remembered, Count Radu was trying to rip her hair out, or rip her face off. A broken memory sparked in her mind. *No...* Radu was dead. She killed him.

That meant she was rich! All of his wealth. His mansion, the lovely pastry foods within it, the carpet, all those people that did what you tell them to do. Where was it?

She jumped to her feet and surveyed the hillside. Rocks. Dirt. A plume of smoke in the distance... rising from a grey city of spires and towers.

The fire.

It was all gone.

There was no need for her to check. The apple tree was telling her. Heard from a snake that had got wind from a rat — before it became lunch — that was told by nature to pass the message on. And the natural world never lied, unlike the druidic council, unlike people. It had no need to, it always won in the end.

Likely a lesson in there somewhere, but for now it was lost on Heather. She slumped against the tree and slid to the ground.

A long, black leg, knuckled and bristling with hairs, reached across her leg. An eight-eyed head forced itself under her arm and rubbed its pedipalps against her lap. She ruffled the space behind the eyes.

"Well, when do we start?" Grog's hand engulfed her shoulder and half her frame as he sat next to her. He gave Legs a pat.

"Start what?" she asked.

"Druid training of course. I'm going to need to show the council something before they sign me up."

"Don't worry about the council," Heather said. "I'll train you my way."

Thanks

Thank you for reading The Unicorn Heist. If you enjoyed this story, please consider leaving a review on Amazon or Goodreads, self-published authors like myself really do rely on your ratings and reviews.

If you'd like to be informed whenever I release a new story, you can sign up to my mailing list at https://dgredd.net.

You may also enjoy these other stories. They are set in the same world as The Unicorn Heist and written in the same style.

You Can't Prevent Prophecy
Old Wizards Home
Harald's Adventure Wares

Here's a little taste of Old Wizards Home:

Rodius Drach glared at his sorrel soup. From around the tin spoon, mushy globules of green glared back. What was it about sorrel soup that put him in such a foul mood? Was it the vacant taste? Chewy texture? Or just the fact that it heralded the arrival of Sixthday evening, which meant only one thing.

"Time for games night, Rodius."

Sister Emerelda swooped through the door with her usual hawkish grace, eyes searching for scurrying prey, mouth pulled back into the veneer of a smile. He knew better than to be taken in by the gentle touch and patient manner of an elf. If he'd had minions half as treacherous, he'd never have failed in his conquest of the The Three Kingdoms.

Light from the small fireplace made Sister Emerelda's silhouette dance around his gilded cage. The wooden bed, table, and chair crowded the room, forcing her to thread through the tight gaps remaining. A light breeze from her passage ruffled his prize possession, a tapestry depicting the height of his power, replete with cowering peasants and bolts of arcane energy.

"Come on, Rodius. Let me help you up."

With his arm now caught in her talons, he let her lead him out from the safety of his cell, into the hall. At least the soup would be discarded before she threw him back... pointy-eared bitch.

An aroma of wooden teeth and boiled cabbage filled the hallway. Everlasting torches dotted the high stone walls, well out of reach of the residents lest they find alternate uses for the magical flames. White gowned brothers, sisters, and assorted laity brisked by, smiles and kind words dripping in their wake. Did they truly think the great Rodius Drach, Archmage of the Glaranox Tower, Possessor of the Telusian Eye, could be deceived so easily? Bah! If only he could escape from their meddlesome anti-magic field...

"Here we are," Sister Emerelda said. "What game would you like to play?"

The common-room had been once again transformed into a menagerie of boredom and pointlessness. A puzzle here, a kings board there, cards by the fireplace. But Rodius knew the real game afoot: doing whatever they could to dull his mind, whittle down his resolve.

He'd never let them win. No, damn it. Rodius Drach would fight tooth and nail until the bitter end. Time was forever on his side. His deal with the Dark Lord promised him that.

"Rodius?" Sister Emerelda tapped his forearm with a claw. "Would you like to have a game of kings with your friend?"

Delevar Godson, the white wizard, was no friend. Already he laid in wait by the kings board, grey hair hanging limp over his weathered face, hands hidden in the folds of his pristine cloak. Rodius jerked his arm free of Sister Emerelda and shooed her away. Even she knew better than to get between he and his nemesis.

"Oh, Rodius." Delevar's high pitched voice was smoothed by the same infuriating calm it held for the past ten thousand years. "Would you like to play a game of kings with me?"

"No I would not!" Rodius held his chin high and looked down upon the lesser wizard. "I challenge you to a magic battle!"

Fire flared deep behind Delevar's eyes. So! The old idiot still had a bit of spark left.

Rodius took two steps back and held his arms out from the layers of robe in readiness. Firelight played in the grout of the flagstone floor, like a powerful magic reaching through the room. Now, with Delevar before him, Rodius could finally slay the man who had brought the Tower down. Revenge was at hand!

The familiar tingle of sorcerous magic welled from deep

within his blackened soul — another gift from the Dark Lord — and pooled in his heart. With a weave of his fingers he constructed the spell, spoke the forbidden tongue, and launched his magic.

Violet and amber sparks blasted the air and winked out of existence almost as soon as they left his outstretched palms.

"Rodius." Sister Emerelda shot up from beside a half-catatonic witch. "No magic. You know the rules. Sit down and enjoy the game with your friend."

"No, damn it." Rodius shuffled around to face her. "I won't be dismissed so easily, wench! If I had my way you would be nothing but one of my concubines, or discarded into my Argal army to be their plaything!"

A murmur from behind punctuated a sudden, stark light. Delevar! Rodius had turned his back on him! Was this it, the final moment before his body was frayed and the bargain struck with the Dark Lord had its last clause enacted?

Sister Emerelda wagged a finger. "Delevar, no magic either. Honestly you two, it's the same every Sixthday. Why don't you both sit—"

"Enough!" Rodius announced. "I demand you release us from this monastery's damned anti-magic field. Become witness to true power the likes of which hasn't been seen in an age!"

"If you two don't sit down and play nice, I'm going to call in Ferelden."

Rodius shambled back to the table, casting a frown over his shoulder at the jailer, and sat down. Patience. That was what was needed, he must remember. He had all the time in the world to wait this purgatory out.

Various mouth-agape faces resumed their previous conversations and time-wasting activities.

"My queen takes your paladin." Delevar's arthritic hand curved into a sickle over the board. He smiled. "Your move."

"Bah!" Rodius sat back and crossed his arms. "Your feeble intellect is no match against mine, Delevar. I have already sat across from you, I won't debase myself any further by playing *games*."

"You're just scared of Ferelden, that's all."

"I am not. He is nothing but a brute." Rodius sniffed and raised his chin higher. "He'd have made an excellent general in my armies."

"Let it go, old man. You haven't had your armies for five elven ages. It's all gone. The Tower, the council, the conquest. Half of what we did is legend now, on its way to become myth."

Rodius leaned over the table and hissed. "Exactly you old fool! The reason for our imprisonment here is forgotten. Soon, they will let down their guard. And then! Then Rodius Drach will command the Armies of Argal once again! Tremble peasants and kings alike!"

"Sit down." Delevar reached an imploring hand out. "You're going to get Ferelden sent over."

"Bah!" Rodius straightened his robes and retook his seat. "You're scared of him too."

"As should every wizard be. Psions are bad news." Delevar glanced at the other elderly captives around them. "And a psion who teams up with the Orydians is even worse news. Something is afoot, Rodius."

With a grunt, Rodius reached toward an obsidian swordsman and attacked the white wizard's army. Patience. Let them believe he was a neutered old mage, incapable of free-thought. Time, as always, was on his side.